Echo

A Kate Redman Mystery: Book 6

Celina Grace

This book is for my friend Helen Watson,
with love and thanks (and bloomers).

Prologue

FOR THREE WEEKS IT HAD rained every day. For those past three weeks, daybreak was a gloomy affair. The skies gradually moved from a thick blanket of dingy white clouds to the deepest shade of grey, peaking here and there in ominous black thunderheads. The rain came down hard in rippling sheets, or softly, insidiously; pattering onto land already sodden, into rivers which threatened to break their weakening banks, onto roofs which leaked and dripped and twice collapsed under the sheer weight of water.

Munford Gorge was a local beauty spot nine miles from the West Country town of Abbeyford. A large lake at the bottom of an encircling bracelet of hills, their steep sides comprised equally of moorland and deciduous forest. On a sunny summer's day, the sandy shore of the lake was swamped with picnicking families, small children running and splashing in the shallow edges of the water, bolder souls venturing out onto the depths on canoes and flotation-devices before their anxious parents called them into shore. On warm summer nights, teenagers built campfires, smoking weed and taking pills, losing their virginity to the lap and swell of the lake waters breaking in wind-ruffled wavelets upon the little beach.

Now, in February, nobody went there. No one save a few hardy walkers, braving the torrential rain, trudging along the shoreline before taking the footpath that led up across the moorland and over the escarpment of the first hill. Now, at midnight, no one went there at all. The wind pushed the surface of the lake into foam-frilled waves which crashed against the wet sand of the banks. Rain poured down relentlessly, hissing against the saturated ground. Puddles became ponds, streams became rivers. Up on the far shore of the lake, as the ground inclined steeply towards the brow of the hill, subterranean groans became louder and louder, until, with a dull roar, a section of the hillside gave way. Mud, rocks and stones rushed downhill in a landslide. The shattered surface of the lake became even more turbulent, as the hillside cascaded into the water.

The rain eased a little, then slackened completely. After the thunder and crash of the last few minutes, the countryside by the lake grew quiet once more, the plink plink of falling drips the only sound to be heard other than the slap of the waves as they broke against new piles of mud and stone where the land had collapsed. Eventually the black clouds above were chased away as the wind strengthened. A thin sliver of moon cast a faint, tremulous radiance over the devastation below it. Even so, there was not enough light to bring a glimmer to the bones that could now be seen, poking out from the tumble of mud, tree-roots and stones that the landslide had brought to the surface.

Old bones are not white. The twisted remnants of what had once been a hand were brown; as brown as the earth that surrounded them. Even if a human observer had been there to watch, they would have seen nothing in the faint light of the moon. The bones stretched forward in darkness, in silent, unseen supplication.

Chapter One

"Okay," Detective Inspector Mark Olbeck said. "So what about *this* one?"

He regarded himself in the mirror anxiously. Such was his focus on the suit he was currently modelling, he failed to notice that his companion had slithered from her chair and was engaged in hiding her head underneath a pile of velvet waistcoats.

"Mark," Kate Redman said, her voice muffled. "It's a grey suit. It's nice. It's as nice as the fifteen other grey suits you've tried on. Can we please just pick one now and go and get a coffee or something?"

"Mmm," said Olbeck, continuing to stare into the mirror. "I don't know about the lapels, though. I mean, they're seventies, but are they too seventies? I don't want to look like an ABBA tribute act or anything."

Kate, head still buried, suppressed a scream. Then, taking a deep breath, she pushed herself out from under the waistcoats and sat up. "Seriously, I had no idea you were going to be such a *girl* about this. Can't you, you know, ask Theo about this? Ask Jeff? Please?"

Olbeck caught her eye in the mirror. "Sorry. Am I being a pain?"

"Yes. Seriously, I know it's your wedding and all, but...Mark, it's a suit. It looks great. Please buy it. Please. Then we can go and do something else. Anything else."

Chuckling, Olbeck turned the collar up and then down again. "Okay. You've persuaded me. I'll buy it."

"Thank God." Kate pretended to swoon in relief.

"Who are you bringing?" Olbeck asked as they made their way to the exit of the department store. A grey and white striped bag with ribbon handles hung from his arm.

"What?"

"Are you bringing anyone to the wedding?" Olbeck asked patiently.

"Oh, God, I don't know," said Kate. They'd reached the pavement outside by now and both grimaced as the rain hit them. Kate fumbled for her umbrella and Olbeck flipped up the hood of his coat. "Stuart, maybe. If his new girlfriend lets him come."

"Are you mad?" asked Olbeck. "We've sent

Stuart his invitation already. He's *bringing* his new girlfriend."

"Oh, bollocks," said Kate. "Oh well. Do I actually have to have an escort? Can't I come on my own?"

"Yes, of course. I just thought you might like to bring someone along, you know, for company."

"Well, thanks," muttered Kate. "I'm sure I'll manage to scrape someone up. Besides, I know loads of people going. I'm sure I'll be fine."

"Mmm." Olbeck paused at the kerbside, hesitating. The rain was coming down so hard, it was difficult to see across the street. "God, this weather. Has it actually stopped raining this *year*?"

Kate said nothing, engaged as she was in crossing the road without being hit by flying sheets of water from passing cars, but she agreed with the sentiment. Had there ever been such a wet start to the year?

They made it to the multi-storey car park where they'd both left their cars. They reached Kate's little Ford first and she fumbled in her handbag for her keys.

"Listen, I need to talk to you about the speech—" she began, before both and Olbeck's mobiles started to ring at the same time. They shared a glance of mutual apprehension before answering their calls.

"Hello, sir—" Kate heard Olbeck say before she heard a familiar voice on the end of her phone line.

"What's up, Rav?"

"Oh, hi, Kate. Did I interrupt you?"

"Only doing some shopping. What's the problem?"

"I'm with the chief now—" Rav began, and as Kate listened, she could hear Olbeck listening to Anderton's voice on his phone in a rather eerie tandem effect, as both men were clearly calling from the same location.

"I'll be right there," Kate heard Olbeck say, just as she was saying, "Fine, Rav, I'll be there as soon as I can."

Olbeck and Kate both terminated their respective calls and turned to one another.

"Here we go again," sighed Olbeck.

"No rest for the wicked," agreed Kate. "That was Anderton, yes?"

"Yes. He's at Munford Gorge, with—"

"Rav," finished Kate. "They've found a body?"

"Yep. That's it."

"Right," said Kate. "So I'm following you, yes? I don't know the way."

It was slow going making their way out of Abbeyford. Kate's windscreen wipers struggled to clear the lashing rain from the glass and, more than once, she lost sight of Olbeck's car as other vehicles overtook her. Eventually, she managed to find her way to the dual carriageway that ran from

Abbeyford towards Bristol. She had a vague idea that Munford Gorge lay on the west side of the town, but where, exactly? She caught sight of Olbeck's car up ahead, parked in the layby, with yellow hazard lights flashing, and breathed a sigh of relief. She pulled in behind him and tooted her horn.

Once out of the city, the traffic eased a little. Kate saw Olbeck's yellow indicator begin flashing and a moment later, saw the brown road sign for Munford Gorge. The two cars drove slowly down a smaller road and then turned again into an unsurfaced track that ended in a small car park. It was full of police vehicles, the white vans of the scene of crime officers and the ambulance that would eventually transport the body to the mortuary to await the post mortem examination.

Kate struggled to pull her already wet coat on. The rain hadn't eased at all – it still fell relentlessly from the sky. Rivulets of muddy water were already flowing across the stony, rutted surface of the car park from the slightly raised ground that lay to its rear. Kate thought of all the trace evidence that was being washed away, even as she and Olbeck made their way to the scene, and frowned. She said as much to her companion.

"I know," said Olbeck. "But what can we do? Let's just hope there's *something* left."

They reached the lakeside and walked towards the bustle of activity at the far end of the lake.

Kate spotted Rav and waved. She was still unused to seeing him back at work. The thought made her smile; she was so pleased that he'd managed to make it back. Rav had been terribly injured in the course of duty two years ago, and Kate knew he'd sometimes wondered whether he would be able to come back at all.

SOCO had already erected the white tent that hid the body from public view; not that there was any public to screen it from – the hissing rain meant that the only people here were professionally involved. Kate, Rav and Olbeck ducked through the entrance flap of the tent and straightened up. Kate's eyes immediately went to the tall figure of Detective Chief Inspector Anderton, who stood looking down at the body. Her first feeling was one of surprise. She'd expected to see a *body* but here, amidst the tumbled earth, was just a sad collection of bones. For a moment, she was reminded of something else, something quite innocuous, but the exact memory eluded her. Then it came to her: a trip to London and to the British Museum, looking at the exhibition of the body found in the peat bog, thousands of years old and still perfectly preserved.

Anderton looked up as they approached. "Morning," he said. "Something slightly out of the ordinary here."

Olbeck crouched down to look more closely. "This is *old*. Isn't it? We're talking years, here."

"Mmm." Anderton made a noise of assent. "I would have thought so."

Kate recollected her first impression. "I suppose it *is* a suspicious death, sir? It's not actually an archaeological find?"

Anderton looked at her briefly and smiled. "I admit the thought did cross my mind, Kate. It's not as if this area isn't thick with historical artefacts – and bones. But, look here—" He crouched down beside Olbeck, pointing, and Rav and Kate leant forward to see. "Look here." His pointing finger indicated a fine metal chain around the base of the skull, too clogged with mud to make out any fine details. "That's modern jewellery. Twentieth century, at least. No, I think we're definitely looking at a job for the team."

Kate ran her gaze over the rest of the body, what she could see of it. Half of the torso was still buried in mud. Now she was closer, she could see slimy scraps of cloth adhering to some of the bones. Was it a man or a woman? An adult at least, she thought, with an inner shiver of something like relief.

"Excuse me, please." They all turned at the sound of the voice. A burly middle-aged man stood behind them, white-suited.

Anderton raised his eyebrows as he rose to his feet. "And you are?"

"Ivor Gatkiss. Pathologist."

"Oh, right." Anderton made a sweeping gesture

with his arm towards the rest of his team. "All right, guys, move back. Let the doc get to work."

They reconvened by the entrance to the tent, nobody suggesting moving outside into the pouring rain. Kate could already see water beginning to trickle under the edges of the tent, running towards the slight hollow in which the skeleton rested. The techs would have to work fast to preserve the scene, she thought. A drop of water fell on the exposed skin on the back of her neck and made her shiver.

"Right," said Anderton. "Now, there's not a lot we can do with this one until we know a bit more about the body. There's no point going back and pulling MISPER records until we know when he or she died, who they might possibly be… you get my drift. Someone needs to stay to see if the techs can give us anything immediate to go on. You never know, there might be a wallet or a handbag buried underneath that lot." He gestured to the sea of mud that surrounded the bones. "Always think positively. So, who's going to stay?"

There was a moment's silence. Kate could feel her own reluctance echoed in both Rav and Olbeck's demeanour. The tent was cold and draughty and her feet were starting to become uncomfortably wet.

"I'll stay," Rav said, after the silence stretched on for an uncomfortable minute too long.

"Oh, no, don't worry. I'll do it," said Kate immediately. Rav still looked so frail she couldn't bear to think of him standing about in this miserable place.

"Well done, Kate," said Anderton, who had clearly been thinking along similar lines. Kate smiled a little, warmed by his approval.

"Thanks," Rav said gratefully. She said goodbye to the three of them and watched them leave. At least I'm in the dry, she told herself, trying to make the best of it. Another drip fell on the back of her neck and she shivered again.

The work inside the tent went on. Kate watched, shifting from numb foot to numb foot, wondering whether there was really any point her being there. She stared at the brown bones protruding from the earth, wondering who they belonged to. The jewellery suggested that the body was female, but not necessarily. How long had it been here? Could it conceivably be a natural death? But then, how had the body been buried? Kate mused, pacing up and down and stamping her feet.

After half an hour, she moved over to where Doctor Gatkiss was still examining the body.

"I don't believe we've met before," said Kate. She was tired of standing about silently.

Doctor Gatkiss looked up and just as quickly looked down again. "No, I don't think we have. I haven't been working at the labs that long." He had a quiet voice and a shy manner that Kate found rather endearing.

"Are you Andrew's replacement? Sorry, Doctor Stanton's replacement, I mean?"

Doctor Gatkiss nodded, with another quick look at her, before turning back to his work.

"How's he getting on?" Kate persisted. She knew Andrew had taken a bit of a career swerve, leaving the pathology labs for a stint on a team with Medicin Sans Frontieres, working in Sierra Leone to try and halt the current Ebola epidemic. Kate and Stanton's relationship was long since over but she couldn't help still worrying about him a little. Kate had finally – reluctantly – joined Facebook and occasionally saw a picture from Andrew's timeline; smiling children in African villages, happy faces under intensely blue skies, but nothing more than that.

"I – I think he's fine. I'm sorry, detective, would you mind – I just have to concentrate—"

"Of course. Sorry." Kate stepped back and let the doctor get back to work. She pushed her cold hands deeper into the pockets of her coat and felt a faint buzz under her fingertips. Her mobile phone, set to vibrate. Clearly it was Anderton or Olbeck wanting an update. She groped for her phone, grabbing it just as it fell silent. Kate pulled it from her pocket and looked at the screen to see who she'd missed.

Doctor Gatkiss concluded his examination and got to his feet, ineffectually trying to brush the mud from the knees of his protective suit. He turned to see Kate staring at her mobile phone screen as if turned to stone, finally frozen into immobility by the biting cold.

"Detective?" he asked tentatively. "Detective?"

Kate gave a start and snapped back to attention. She put the phone back in her pocket and turned her gaze on him, forcing a rictus smile. "I'm so sorry. You wanted me?"

She could see that Doctor Gatkiss had an inkling that her full attention was not immediately on him, but he obviously decided to speak anyway. "I've finished the preliminary examination. I'm afraid that I can't give you any firm indication on cause of death yet. I believe the body to be that of a young woman, possibly late teens, early twenties, but there will need to be a post mortem before I can give you any other information." Kate nodded, unsurprised. Doctor Gatkiss continued. "You may actually need the services of a specialist forensic anthropologist. These remains have been here for years. Most probably decades."

"Right," Kate said. The small part of her mind that was always focused on her work came to the fore, leaving the rest of her brain in utter turmoil. "Thanks very much. We'll speak later, I'm sure."

She watched the pathologist leave the tent, the movement of the entrance flap momentarily showing the driving rain that still continued to pour down outside. Kate stared blindly after him for a moment and then turned back. She conferred briefly with the senior investigating officer, Stephen Smithfield, going through the motions, working on autopilot. Then she left the tent herself, slogging back to her car through the mud and the rain, head down, almost oblivious to the discomfort.

Once she was in the driving seat, her wet coat flung into the back of the car, the engine running and the heater turned up to full, Kate drew her phone from her pocket again and stared at it. She hadn't been mistaken, then. She hadn't hallucinated it. *Mary Redman*, the screen said, showing the telephone number from which the call had been missed. Kate looked at her mother's name, the words blurring a little as her hand shook. She hadn't spoken to her mother in almost five years. She looked at the name a moment longer and then tossed the phone in the back seat, clamping her teeth together as she put the car in gear and prepared to drive away.

Chapter Two

INCREDIBLY, THE NEXT MORNING WAS a sunny one. The rainclouds temporarily vanished and the sky stretched across the horizon like a gauzy blue blanket, fuzzed here and there with wispy white clouds. Kate sat eating her breakfast in dancing sunbeams, occasionally deliberately moving her head forward so that the dazzle forced her to shut her eyes. She moved her face from side to side in the unexpected warmth, knowing that it wouldn't last.

Her mobile phone lay beside her plate. Every so often, she picked it up to look again at the list of missed calls. *Mary Redman*. Kate read the name and then placed the phone back down on the table with an exclamation of annoyance. What did it mean? Why was her estranged mother trying to call her?

Could it have been a mistake? Mary's phone tumbled about in the bottom of a handbag, unlocked, Kate's number accidentally pressed? It was that thought that stopped Kate doing the obvious thing and ringing her mother back – that and the realisation that she had absolutely no idea what she would say. What could you say to a mother who hadn't wanted to talk to you for half a decade? Put like that, Kate's mood dimmed further, despite the cheerful sunshine. She put the phone in her handbag and sat back down at the kitchen table, chewing her toast moodily.

The squeak and crash of the cat flap, recently installed in the back door, heralded the arrival of the newest occupant of Kate's household, padding over the kitchen tiles before appearing with a leap into Kate's lap. Merlin pushed his big black head up under Kate's chin insistently, until she gave in and began stroking him. Soon, he curled himself into a comma shape on Kate's lap, purring in satisfaction. He was so big that he drooped over each of her legs, but it didn't seem to bother him.

"Don't get comfortable," Kate warned him. "I've got to leave for work in five minutes." Merlin gave a lazy flick of the ear in response.

"You do realise you've become the biggest cliché in the book?" Kate's brother Jay had told her, a grin in his voice, when she'd told him she'd got a cat. They were talking on the phone at the time so Kate was forced to actually *tell* him she was giving him the finger in response, which somewhat robbed the gesture of its power.

For a moment, Kate thought of ringing Jay there and then, to see if he'd heard from their mother or if he knew why Mary Redman had inexplicably decided to ring her. But as she brought up his number, she reconsidered. He'd be on his way to work right now which meant he'd probably be underground, stuck on a tube train somewhere in West London, and out of mobile signal. And what if it *had* been a mistake on her mother's part? No, best to leave it.

Kate thought of her little brother as she started the car. Jay and his long-term girlfriend, Laura, had moved to London last summer, having both managed to obtain quite impressive jobs in media and in finance respectively. Kate was proud of Jay – she was proud of them both – but she missed them. Until last July, they'd only been a ten minute drive away. Now she didn't have any family left in Abbeyford at all. Inevitably, her thoughts snapped back to her mother's phone call. At the same time, she became aware that the sunshine had gone, the blue sky blotted out by ominous looking black clouds. As Kate drove within sight of Abbeyford Police Station, the first few drops of rain began to fall, spattering her windscreen.

Kate paused in the doorway to the office, as she tended to these days. It was still something of a shock, but a pleasant one, to see Rav back at his desk. And of course there was the new DC, recently arrived from Cheltenham. Felicity Durrant. "Call me Fliss," was the first thing she'd said on arrival, with the kind of ringing self-confidence you'd expect to find in a baronet's daughter, not a recently qualified detective constable. Kate liked her – you couldn't help *liking* her – but found her rather annoying too. Keep a grip on it, Kate reminded herself. She knew she had a tendency to take against people far too quickly – look at how she'd first reacted to Stuart, for example, and now he was one of her closest friends. At least this time she was more aware of the fact, and was able to pull herself up on it, every time she felt as if she were falling into bad habits. She didn't think Fliss (stupid name!) had noticed. She wasn't the sensitive type.

"Morning, Kate," Fliss sing-songed across the desk as Kate sat down. "Shame about the sunshine. Still, it was nice while it lasted. I heard about the body at Munford Gorge, that's a bit of a turn-up for the books, isn't it? Jane said it was ancient. I suppose we'll hear about it from the boss today. Can I get you a coffee?"

Kate thought longingly of the days when Theo used to sit across from her and the only greeting she'd get first thing was a comment when she looked particularly haggard. She glanced across to where Theo sat now, three desks over. He and Rav were looking at something on Rav's phone, laughing. "That would be great, thanks, Fliss," she said, finally, trying to sound grateful.

She turned on her computer and began the process of easing into her working day, checking her emails, listening to her voicemails, riffling through the paperwork that needed her attention. Fliss's hand appeared in front of her suddenly, bearing a steaming cup of coffee and making Kate jump. "Here you go!"

"Thanks," Kate muttered. She took a sip, burning her lip, and put the cup down hurriedly. Behind her she heard the office door crash back against the wall and realised Anderton, her boss, had made his characteristic entrance.

"Morning, team. I hope you're feeling mean and keen and ready to get on with some work?"

"I'm definitely feeling mean," said Kate, turning around.

Anderton grinned at her. "Glad to hear it, Kate. Hope you didn't catch cold from your vigil yesterday."

"I'll survive—" Kate began and was surprised by an enormous sneeze.

Anderton raised his eyebrows. "Oh, dear. Get yourself a hot drink." He glanced at the steaming mug beside her and added "Oh, you have. Well, never mind."

By this time, everyone had turned from their phones, computers and newspapers and were facing their boss, who began his usual pacing up and down the room as he began to recap what they knew.

"Now, unusually," Anderton began, "we don't actually have a starting point for this investigation yet. Without knowing the age, sex or ethnicity of the victim, we're a bit stymied on moving forward." He looked hopefully at Kate. "Anything you can enlighten us on, Kate?"

Kate sneezed again. "Sorry. Yes, there is some preliminary data. The doctor thought the victim was female and young, late teens or early twenties. That was about all he was able to tell me."

"No idea how long she'd been in the ground?"

Kate shook her head. "He didn't say. I guess we'll know more after the PM."

Anderton nodded. "Indeed. That's taking place tomorrow. Kate, could you be our representative?"

Kate groaned. "Why is it always *me* who has to do the PMs?"

"Because you love them," Anderton said, grinning.

"That's totally untrue. You make me sound like a complete ghoul."

Fliss looked back and forth between Kate and Anderton, as if she couldn't quite believe her ears. She was still treating the DCI with the hushed reverence of a lowly cleric for the head bishop, or perhaps the Pope. Kate smiled inwardly.

Anderton rubbed his chin. "All right, you're off post mortem duty. Theo, you do it."

"Oh, *cheers*," Theo said.

"It's all right," Rav said. "I'll do it. I need to get back into the swing of things."

"Good lad," Anderton said. "All right. We'll see what the PM throws up, if anything. We might need a specialist, a forensic anthropologist or something similar. Felicity, that's a job for you. Could you do some research and get me a few names? The path labs will be able to advise." Fliss virtually stood to attention, which made Kate smile again. "Kate, it might be worth you going through the MISPER files for young women who've been reported missing."

"No problem," Kate said. "But do we know the date range? I mean, how far back do you want me to go?"

Anderton shrugged. "Your guess is as good as mine. Why not start with this year, and work backwards as far as you can by the end of the day? Tomorrow we might have a better idea of when our victim was actually killed."

"If she *was* killed," said Olbeck.

"True. But natural deaths don't tend to end up with the bodies being buried in out of the way beauty spots. She didn't dig herself into the ground."

Kate watched Anderton as he paced up and down. She tested herself for romantic feelings towards him and was pleased to find that they'd reduced to a mere glimmer. Was she finally free of her attraction to him? Was she *finally* free? She took a deep, relieved breath. One less complication in her life, at least. Now she could reap the benefits of finally controlling her feelings. It had been hard

– so hard – to suppress what she felt for Anderton, but she'd fought it every step of the way and now it seemed it had been a battle worth winning.

She returned to her desk as the briefing broke up. The sight of her handbag on the floor by her chair recalled the missed telephone call from her mother and her high spirits suddenly fell. Why had her mother called her? She scrolled through until she found the missed number. I'll call her later, she thought, putting off the evil deed, wondering whether she'd actually go through with it.

She began working through the reports of missing young women. It was a quicker task than she'd anticipated. This year, in Abbeyford and its surrounding districts, only five young women had been reporting missing. Two were assumed to be runaways from a local care home. The other three seemed equally straightforward – one was a young woman with a history of mental health problems, last seen in the vicinity of the Severn Bridge, a notorious suicide spot. Kate sighed. The other two young women who'd been reported missing had both been found safe and well. She finished reading and shuffled the papers into a neat pile. It didn't seem likely that the body would belong to someone who'd only gone missing in the last year. Surely the bones would have had to have been buried for much longer? How long did it actually take for a body to become a skeleton? Kate tapped her pencil on her chin and thought for a moment, reaching for her desk phone a moment later.

"Hi, Steven. It's Kate Redman. Could I ask you a quick question?"

One blessing, when it came to the senior investigating officer of the local SOCO team, thought Kate, was that he was never fazed by any question to do with forensics. Steven Smithfield simply assumed that you felt the same keen, some might say slightly worryingly, obsessive interest that he had for his subject.

"It varies completely," was his answer to Kate's question. "Dependent on a multitude of factors. How wet the ground was, whether there was any insect activity, you could have saponification, adverse weather conditions, all sorts of things might affect the rate of decay."

"Fine, fine," said Kate, rolling her eyes. "But could you give me a ballpark figure? I mean, are we talking weeks? Months? Or would it take years?"

"Totally depends on the conditions," said Steven. "Could be three months, could be three years. I couldn't say."

How helpful. Kate sighed and was about to terminate the call when Steven spoke up. "Is this about that body we found at Munford Gorge?"

No, I routinely ring up to ask about the skeletonisation of a human body, Steven. Just for kicks. Kate thought it but didn't say it. She answered his question in the affirmative.

"Well, if it's *that* one we're talking about, we're definitely looking at years. What did I say earlier? Three years? I'd take that as a starting point. Three years or older."

Kate clenched a fist in triumph but kept her voice level. "That's great, Steven, thanks. Really helpful."

"You're welcome."

Three years or older. Well, that was a start. Kate fired up the database again and began to check reports from three years ago. Perhaps she ought to do two years ago, just in case she missed something important. She went and got herself another coffee and sat down to her desk again, feeling re-energised. Absorbed in her work, her mother's missed phone call went totally out of her head.

Chapter Three

"Who's that from?"

Kate looked up at the sound of Theo's voice. "What's that?"

Theo pulled Fliss's empty chair out from under her desk and sat down opposite Kate. "Your card. Who's it from?"

Kate's glance fell to the flowery card in her hand. She smiled. "It's from Rosa. Remember her?" Theo looked blank. "From last year. You know, the drugs case?"

"Oh, yeah. She's writing to you?"

"We write to each other, occasionally. I just like to – to keep her spirits up."

Theo looked unconvinced. "Oh, yeah?"

Kate looked down at the card and the hesitant writing inside of it. "She's doing okay. In an open prison now and she's gone through rehab. Hopefully she'll make it, once she gets out."

"Yeah," said Theo once more, with finality.

He was clearly sorry he'd asked. "Anyway, what's happening today?"

"Rav's at the PM so hopefully he'll come back with a bit more info. I'm still going through the missing persons reports. Not sure it's really worth my while until we get an actual date of death."

"True." Theo yawned. "Why do I get the feeling that this is going to be one of *those* cases?"

"What do you mean?" asked Fliss, who'd just returned to her desk with a steaming mug in her hand. Courteously, Theo stood up to let her sit down.

"Oh, you know. One of those cases that drags on and on and *on* and we never find out who did it or even who the vic was."

Kate spluttered. "We've never even had *one* case like that here, Theo. What are you talking about?"

"There's always a first time," Theo said darkly.

Felicity was looking puzzled. "Didn't you have an unidentified body last year?"

Kate nodded. "Yes, the body we found in a derelict cottage. Badly decomposed – we had to go on dental records and DNA. But we found him all right. John Henry Miller. We had to do some digging to identify him but we *did* identify him. Just as we're going to do on this case." She shot Theo a glance, daring him to disagree, but he was already making his way back to his desk, his back turned. Felicity nodded, a serious look on her face, before she turned her attention to her own computer screen.

Gradually, quiet settled over the room as they all began to work, the silence punctuated at intervals by ringing telephones, the buzz and whirr of the coffee machine and the click and squeak of the office door as people came and went. Kate finished checking her emails and looked over at Theo.

"By the way, are you taking anyone to Mark's wedding?"

"Huh?" Theo asked absently, intent on his work.

"Are you taking anyone to Mark's wedding?"

Theo looked up. He smiled. "Oh, that. Well, I've narrowed it down to a choice of three. Still deciding."

Kate snorted. She might have known. "Right you are."

"Why?" asked Theo, still grinning. "Want me to be your date?"

Kate flicked a rubber band at him. "No. I just wondered if I was going to be the only one going on my own."

"I'll be your plus one if you like," said Fliss, with rather too much enthusiasm for Kate's liking. "We could make a girls night of it!"

Kate forced a smile. "That's something to bear in mind. Thanks, Fliss."

"It's *no* problem."

Oh, God. Kate slumped over her keyboard,

moodily clicking the mouse. She found Fliss particularly irritating this morning. Her innate sense of fair play meant she was also irritated with herself because she was being rather unfair. Fliss wasn't doing anything wrong. She couldn't help being so damn annoying.

Kate got up and made herself another coffee. Glancing at the clock on the wall by the water heater, she realised that the post mortem on the remains would now be underway. Despite her protests to Anderton yesterday, she thought then that she would rather have attended. At least then she'd know more before anyone else and perhaps have some idea as to how they could progress the case further. Theo's doom-laden sentiments reoccurred to her. *One of those cases...* Kate dismissed such gloomy thoughts. They had the sex, the rough age, presumably a full set of teeth with which to compare dental records. There was that necklace that Anderton had noticed. Other identifying objects may have been buried with the body, not to mention the possibility of clothes and shoes. They had plenty to be going on with, Kate told herself as she sat back down. Plenty. She kept glancing at the clock, despite those sentiments, wondering when Rav would be back.

As it turned out, it was past lunchtime when Rav finally returned from the post mortem. Anderton joined the rest of the team in the office while Rav gave them a rundown of what the pathologist had told him. "There's no discernible cause of death, apparently. No obvious knife damage to the bones, nothing left behind that could have been a weapon."

Anderton paced his usual pathway from the whiteboards to the nearest desk and back. "That's not surprising. Anything else?"

Rav flipped the pages of his notebook over and scanned his writing. "Strangulation is a possibility but again, only a possibility. The bones had been tumbled about in the landslide so damage to the hyoid bone could have been caused by that, rather than by human activity."

Anderton nodded. "Again, not a surprise. Any form of identification found?"

"There were some scraps of clothing but most of it had rotted away. We might be able to trace the manufacturers of the underwear. That was synthetic and seems to have stood up to the elements a bit better than her outer clothing. There'll be photos in the main report."

Kate raised a hand. "What about the necklace, Rav?"

Rav smiled. "Now that is the one bit of good news. I took a copy of the photo of the necklace. Here you go—"

He handed it to Kate first who took a good look. Cleaned of the clotting mud, she could clearly see the metal lettering that formed part of the gold chain. "Jonie?," she murmured, almost to herself, reading it.

There was a subdued buzz of excitement. People crowded around the photograph, looking at the necklace which spelt out a girl's name.

"Now *that* is a big step forward," Anderton said. "Possibly. Of course, we're jumping to conclusions that 'Jonie' is the name of the victim. Most people who buy a necklace that spells out a name buy one that spells out their own name, don't they? But not necessarily. It might be the name of our victim's mother, or daughter, or friend."

"Or lover," Olbeck said.

Anderton acknowledged the suggestion with a wave of his hand. "Indeed. Anyway, it's something to go on. We need to try and trace the manufacturer. Fingers crossed it was a bespoke necklace. That really *would* be a stroke of luck..." He trailed off, rubbing his chin. "Rav, what about the age of the bones? That's going to be crucial."

Rav looked a little uncomfortable. "Sorry, guv, they couldn't tell. Doctor Gatkiss said it was a job for a specialist. They're going to send them off to the Centre for Human Anatomy and Human Identification. You know, CAHID, up in Dundee."

"When will they have the results?"

"Not sure. Within the week, I think he said."

"Fine. Keep on at them. Without a definite date, it's going to be ten times harder to ascertain identity." Anderton stopped pacing. "Right, we've got a bit more to go on. Kate, can you narrow down your database searches for anyone with the name 'Jonie' or variations thereof. Different spellings, you know the sort of thing. Abbreviations. Try 'Joan' as well."

"Of course," Kate said.

"Fliss, can you start digging into possible manufacturers for that type of necklace? Anything you can pull up on possible designers, sellers, anything really."

"Yes, sir." Fliss sat up so straight she almost vibrated. Kate hid a grin.

"Rav, keep me posted on updates from the path labs, will you? Chase them if they start slacking off. Mark, have you got five minutes for a quick chat?" Olbeck nodded. "Great, let's wrap it up for now."

The office door crashed shut behind Anderton and Olbeck as they left the room. Kate turned back to her desk and then noticed that Theo, Fliss and Jane were still poring over the picture of the necklace. She went over and joined them.

"People don't wear this kind of stuff now, do they?" Theo mused. As one, they all looked at Fliss as the youngest member of the group.

"Well, *I* wouldn't wear it," she said brightly.

"But would your friends?" asked Kate. "I mean, it's not fashionable to wear name necklaces now, is it?" She was suddenly acutely aware that she sounded middle-aged and out of touch. "It's not, is it?"

Jane was shaking her head. "I used to have one, back in the nineties. It was around the time of *Sex in the City*, remember? Carrie Bradshaw used to wear one."

"Who?" asked Theo. The two older women exchanged amused glances.

"Never mind," said Kate. She looked again at the photograph. "Were necklaces like that around before the nineties?"

Nobody knew. There was a moment's silence and then Theo handed the picture to Fliss. "Here you go."

They drifted back to their respective desks. Kate fired up the database that she'd been searching before and began typing in 'Jonie' with renewed enthusiasm. Theo's previously Cassandra-like proclamations began to fade away in her memory. Perhaps this would be an easy case after all.

Chapter Four

KATE OPENED HER FRONT DOOR that evening to Merlin's frantic mews. He immediately began curling himself around her ankles like black smoke. He was clearly, in his own mind, in imminent danger of starving to death.

"Oh, calm down," said Kate, bending down to stroke him. "Stop panicking."

How nice it was to have someone to greet you when you got home, she thought as she opened a tin of cat food. Even if that someone had four legs and a tail. *I should have got a pet years ago*. Perhaps they should be standard issue for all new police officers – especially single ones.

She put a frozen pizza in the oven to cook, showered, changed into her pyjamas and settled onto the sofa with a newly satiated Merlin curled up on her lap. Kate was tired but not tired enough to go to bed yet. She thought about ringing Jay and then about ringing Hannah, her best friend, and dismissed both ideas – too late. She'd try them tomorrow. The sight of her mobile phone on the coffee table brought her mother's missed call to her mind and as she picked up the phone she realised she'd missed another call. This time, she didn't recognise the number. Could it be her mother again, calling from another line? Did she think that Kate was screening her calls? Kate hesitated, her finger on the redial button. It was probably nothing to do with her mother. A wrong number, perhaps. Kate heard the beep of the oven timer go and got up, carefully dislodging Merlin. Oh well, she wouldn't be calling anyone back tonight, it was almost eleven o'clock. Far too late for making phone calls.

Perhaps it was the pizza, eaten too hastily, or perhaps the puzzle of the mystery mobile number, but whatever it was, Kate slept badly. She woke to the blare of her alarm clock with a curse and stumbled into the bathroom. She was due to pick up Rav on her way to work – he was still not able to drive himself – and she knew she'd be late. She sent a quick and apologetic text before hurrying to get ready.

When she drew up outside of Rav's flat, he was waiting on the pavement, an umbrella over his head to fend off the inevitable raindrops.

"You idiot, why didn't you wait inside?" Kate asked as she opened the passenger door for him.

"Oh, it's all right. I get fed up being indoors, to be honest. I was stuck in there for so long without being able to get out." Rav settled himself carefully into the seat and winced minutely as he reached for the seat belt.

"You okay?" Kate asked anxiously.

"I'm fine," Rav said impatiently. Kate was reminded of her own recovery from an injury, years ago now, and how irritating she used to find everyone's concern.

"Sorry," she said. They drove in silence for a few moments.

"I've got physio later," Rav said after a minute or two. "You remember the physiotherapist? Gill Becker?"

Kate grimaced. "The memories are burned on my brain."

Rav grinned. "She said to say hello, last time I saw her."

"Hmmm." Kate drew up to a T-junction and waited for a gap in the traffic. Rav's mention of his physio session had reminded her that she had her own appointment to go to that week. She had her monthly session with Magda booked in for Friday evening and hoped that work would allow her to attend it. She'd missed a few sessions lately, and Magda had told her that kind of thing wouldn't help her therapy. Apparently the sessions were very carefully structured.

Once they got to the office, Kate familiarised herself with the reports she'd printed out yesterday.

She'd gone through the entire list of missing females from the last twenty years, checking for the name 'Jonie' or variations of the same, looking at the names, the ages and the gender. So far, she'd not come across one exact match – there wasn't anyone called Jonie reported missing in the area from the past two decades. Kate shuffled the papers into a neater pile, thinking. What if the body had been brought from another county? Another country, even? Thinking of it like that, it did seem like a rather hopeless task. Kate mentally squared her shoulders and bent to her keyboard again.

She heard the muffled buzzing of her phone in her bag and groped for it, reaching it just as the ringing stopped. She looked at the call display – again, it was an unfamiliar number. As Kate frowned, thinking, the little icon that denoted a voicemail waiting popped up on the screen. She dialled in to her mailbox and listened. A man's voice, unfamiliar to her. "Hi, Ms. Redman, this is Tin Johnson. You won't know me but I'm a freelance journalist and I'm working on a story that I think you might be able to help me with. I'm also calling on behalf of your mother, Mrs Mary Redman. It's probably easiest to talk about this face to face, or at least on the phone, so do you think you could give me a call back when convenient? Thanks very much." His voice went on to leave a mobile number, repeated twice. Then he said, "Thanks again, goodbye," and there was the click as he disconnected the call.

Kate blinked. She listened to the call again. What the *hell*? She listened to the call once more, from the beginning. There were so many questions she wasn't sure which one was most pertinent. Who was this Tin – *Tin*? Surely she'd misheard, it must have been Tim – Johnson. A journalist? What story? And what the hell was he doing calling on behalf of her *mother*? Kate slowly put her phone down on her desk, staring at it, unseeing, while a thousand different thoughts flew round her head. She thought of the other men her mother had been involved with. Was that what Tim Johnson had meant? He was in a relationship with her mother? What the hell...

Kate slowly became aware that someone was speaking to her. She looked up with a start to see Fliss standing by her desk, patiently repeating herself for what was possibly the fifth time.

"What's that?"

"Do you want another cup of tea?" Fliss asked.

"Um. No." Kate got up and grabbed her phone off the desk. "Thank you," she added, belatedly.

She walked back through the station, out through the main reception and onto the steps outside the main entrance. For once it wasn't raining, although the sky sagged with heavy grey clouds. Kate stood for a moment, irresolute, and then walked quickly down the steps, following the road until she came to the little park five minutes away. She passed through the gateway and kept going until she found a bench towards the middle of the park. The traffic noise was muted there and there was no one else around, no one in the park at all, in fact. The bench was soaking wet, bejewelled with fat beads of water. Kate propped herself against the damp bark of a beech tree and took a deep breath. She dialled the number Tim – was it Tim? – Johnson had left her.

He answered almost immediately.

"Ms Redman? Hi, thanks for calling back."

"No problem," said Kate automatically. "I'm a bit – I don't really know how I can help you."

"Yes, I know my message was a bit mysterious," Tim Johnson said cheerily. He had a nice voice, warm and friendly, and cultured without being what Kate, despite herself, would have called 'posh'. "It's probably easiest if we do meet face to face but I'll fill you in as best I can."

"You were calling about my mother—" Kate began.

"Yes, I understand that you haven't had much contact with Mary over the past few years." He managed to sound sympathetic without sounding patronising, quite a difficult feat. "It's not my business to go into why that is but all I can say to start with is that she would like to see you. I think – did she try and call you?"

"Yes," said Kate. "But I missed the call. I wasn't sure – I wasn't sure whether it was a mistake or not." Why was she telling this complete stranger this? She closed her mouth over the rest of the words that she wanted to say.

"Yes, I can see that. I've been – Mary and I have been collaborating on a feature I'm working on, about the Marhaven care home, the unmarried mothers' home? You know, in Bristol?"

"Sorry," said Kate, at a total loss. "I'm not sure what you mean—"

"Never mind, I can understand you're not familiar with it. Listen, could we actually meet up? It would be much easier to talk in person, explain everything if you see what I mean."

"Okay," said Kate rather feebly. She felt dizzy. It was easiest just to agree.

"Oh, great. How about tomorrow night? Would that suit you?"

"Um. Yes."

"Great. How about we meet at The Black Cat? You know it? It's on the high street, a nice quiet bar so we can talk and it does good food. How about eight o'clock?"

"Okay," said Kate. She had a feeling she should be saying something else but couldn't think what.

"Great. I'll look forward to it. You've got my number so if anything comes up just send me a text and we can rearrange, okay?"

"Great," said Kate in a whisper. Tim Johnson said a cheery goodbye and the line cut off.

Kate pulled the phone away from her head and stared at it blankly. What on Earth had she just got herself into? Who was this Tim Johnson anyway? What feature? What did it have to do with her mother? Kate pressed her clenched fist against her forehead. This was all she needed. Why the bloody hell had she called him back? What was this all *about*?

She made a mammoth effort and brought her fizzing head under control. A few deep breaths, that was the thing... There was no point stressing over what on Earth this was all about when she would find out tomorrow anyway. She was meeting him in a public place, so she wasn't so worried about her personal safety. She might do a quick search on his name when she got back to the station - just to be on the safe side. Should she ring her mother and find out more? No, Kate told herself decisively. *You'll find out tomorrow. Wait until then and then you can decide what to do.*

She turned slowly and made her way to the exit. It had begun to rain again, lightly and then with increasing force, the drops pattering down, adding to the already large puddles. Kate hunched her shoulders against the rain, almost oblivious. Despite her best intentions, she was still thinking about the phone call.

Chapter Five

KATE HAD NEVER BEEN TO The Black Cat before. She didn't really go to bars, not being much of a drinker. Slanting her umbrella back so she could check she was at the right place, she caught sight of the sign; the lettering in a vintage-type font, the black cat of the name painted in a stylised manner, its long tail curving to underline the words. Momentarily, the cat reminded her of Merlin. The Black Cat was a small place, situated in one of the older buildings on the high street. Black-framed, many-paned windows shone with a warm golden light, and inside Kate could see a variety of comfortable looking sofas as well as a small restaurant section. What did this Tim Johnson look like? Kate put down her umbrella and stepped into the foyer of the building, furling the dripping umbrella and shaking out her hair. She'd come straight from work and was dressed in her usual black suit. She was glad, as it felt like armour.

The bar wasn't busy. Kate swept her gaze over

the room. There were a few small groups of people, several couples and a few men on their own, reading newspapers or peering at their phones. Kate wondered which one was Tim Johnson. I should have asked him to wear a red carnation, she thought and, despite the tension, grinned to herself.

A tall man with a rugby player's build turned and caught Kate's eye. He raised his eyebrows in a questioning kind of way and came towards her.

"Kate?"

"Yes," said Kate confusedly. She hadn't expected him to be black. Why not, Kate, she asked herself. A secondary thought came that she also hadn't expected him to be quite so good looking. She took a grip on herself. "Hi. Is it Tim?"

"Tin, actually. It really is Tin." He smiled as she stuttered out an apology. "Don't worry, everyone gets it wrong. Seriously, everyone. It's short for Tindebaye, so you can see why I use an abbreviation."

They made their way to the bar and Tin turned to her to ask what she wanted to drink. He asked for her lemonade without comment and ordered a glass of red wine for himself. Kate waited with him, feeling pleasantly dwarfed. She liked tall men. *Get a grip, she ordered herself. Don't forget what you're here for.*

"'Tindebaye'?" Kate asked as they seated themselves near the fireplace. It was a real fire, another point in this bar's favour. Kate thought she might come here again, it was so nice.

"My mum wanted me to have an African name. I like it, actually, I just got tired of having to spell it out all the time." Tin took a sip of his drink and then sat forward. "Thanks so much for coming to meet me. It must have been a bit confusing for you."

"Well, you could say that."

Tin nodded, looking serious. "As I said, I'm a journalist. Freelance, now. I've worked for some of the nationals but I also do quite a lot for the local papers in the South West." He reached into the back pocket of his jeans and extracted a card which he held out to Kate. "Those are my other contact details and some links to my articles, if you want some more reassurance."

Kate took the card and turned it over in her fingers. There was a QL code on the back and a list of email and social media addresses. She didn't mention that she'd already searched for his name on both the public search engines and various police databases and found nothing alarming. "I'm sure I'd be satisfied with your *bona fides* but..."

"'But what's it got to do with you?'" Tin smiled again. He had the kind of smile that lit up his face. Kate found herself smiling back, unselfconsciously. "Good question. I take it from our phone call earlier that you haven't heard about the Marhaven care home? No?" Kate shook her head. "No, well, most people haven't. Anyway, it's due to be demolished in a couple of weeks, and I pitched the idea for a feature about its history to the editor at the Western Telegraph. She liked it so I started chasing up some details." He paused and gestured to Kate's empty glass, which she had emptied in nervous gulps. "Can I get you another one of those?"

"My round," said Kate. She went and fetched them both another drink and sat back down again.

"So anyway, the Marhaven home has quite a history. It was originally built as a school back in Edwardian times, but in the seventies it was a care home for teenage girls, girls who were what they used to call 'unmarried mothers'. Not just pregnant teenagers, actually, some other girls who were in care, orphans, foster children, that sort of thing."

"Right," Kate said, feeling that she should be making some sort of contribution.

"I put an ad out asking anyone who'd been at the home or who knew anything about it to get in touch and that's when your mum contacted me."

"My mum?" Kate said, blankly. "What's it got to do with her?"

Tin gave her a strange look, half disbelieving, half sympathetic. "Well, she was there, of course. In the home. When she was a teenager. Did she never tell you about it?"

Kate dropped her gaze to the shimmering surface of her glass of lemonade. Her face felt hot.

51

No, her mother had never mentioned anything to her about being in a care home. Being in a care home as a teenager, no less. Kate sifted back through her memories, to her childhood; there had been her older siblings – half siblings – Terry and Amanda, but they'd been removed into care themselves before Kate was born. After that, their contact with Mary had been sporadic and Kate had grown up never really knowing her older brother and sister. Terry had been killed in a motorbike accident at eighteen, and Amanda – Manda, they always called her – had long since moved away. She lived up north now, Kate recalled, and was married with several children. Kate hadn't seen or heard from her in years.

She came back to reality with a start, realising she'd been silent for a good few minutes. Tin was looking at her with a sympathetic look on his face.

"Sorry," said Kate. "You've probably already guessed that my family and I aren't that close. Well, I mean, I'm not that close with some members of it." She thought of Jay, and Courtney and Jade, with affection. "If you've been in contact with my mum, no doubt she's given you her side of the story."

Tin was twirling his half empty glass between his fingers, the liquid within rocking gently up the curved sides of the bowl. "You might be surprised," he said. "But we can talk about that later."

Kate looked at him, curious. "What's she been

saying about me?" Then she realised she didn't really want this handsome man to have to repeat what was bound to have been unflattering. "Never mind. I'd rather not know." She took another sip of her drink. "So is there a story around the care home or are you doing a historical piece? Or something else?"

Tin's cheerful face suddenly looked a little grimmer. "Something else, all right." He put his glass down. "I don't know if you've been following the news lately?"

"When I can."

"You probably know that the digging up of historic abuse cases is the hot topic in journalism right now." Tim paused for a moment and half smiled. "Hot topic or hot potato, I'm not sure which. Anyway, in the light of stuff like Operation Yewtree, Rotherham, etcetera, there's been quite a lot of interest from editors in chasing up stories that might be along a similar line."

Kate was conscious of a slow, sinking feeling. "You're telling me the Marhaven care home was – that there was abuse going on there?"

Tin shrugged. "That, Kate, is the story. Was there? Or wasn't there? There's nothing but rumours and innuendo. Nothing but gossip. The few people I've tried to talk to about it insist they don't know anything – either that or there's nothing there to know. Every time I think I'm getting somewhere I keep coming up against a dead end."

"Okay," Kate said slowly. "So why bother pursuing it?"

Tin sat forward. "*Because* I keep coming up against a dead end. I don't know, call it a hunch, call it intuition, call it sheer bloody-mindedness, but I think there's something there. No one will talk to me, I can't seem to get any further forward, but – I don't know – I don't want to give up just yet."

Kate was thinking. "I thought you said that no one was talking to you. What about my mother?"

"She's talking to me," said Tin.

"Why?" demanded Kate. "What's so different about her? Why is she talking and yet nobody else is?"

Tin sat back again, looking slightly uncomfortable. "Well – special circumstances. It's a bit difficult – I mean, perhaps you should hear it from her."

"Hear what?" asked Kate.

Tin's gaze moved from her face to glance up, over her shoulder. "Perfect timing. You can ask her yourself."

Kate froze. Behind her, over the subdued hubbub of the bar, she could hear the squeak of the main door as it opened and a waft of cold night air as it shut. There were hesitant footsteps behind her that faltered to a stop. Kate hadn't yet looked around.

"Hi, Mary," said Tin, slightly too heartily. "Come and sit down."

Kate remained seated and facing forward. She felt as if she'd frozen in that position, doomed to remain there forever. There was a rustle of clothing and a harsh cough and then Mary Redman sat down at the table, next to Tin and opposite Kate.

Kate looked up and received her second major shock of the evening. What had happened to her mother? Mary Redman was desperately thin, almost skeletal, just a jumble of skin-wrapped bones in her winter coat. There was a bright blue scarf wrapped around her throat and the colour seemed to do something dreadful to the skin of her face, draining it of colour, casting grey shadows underneath her eyes. Kate hadn't seen her mother for almost five years but surely that length of time was not enough to lay such waste to her physically? Kate swallowed hard, knowing that the first flinch when she'd seen her mother had been obvious to both Mary and to Tin.

The silence stretched on. Eventually Mary coughed again, covering her mouth with bony fingers, and then smiled tremulously.

"Sight for sore eyes, aren't I?"

Kate was still staring. From somewhere deep within, she managed to get a grip on herself and pulled her horrified gaze from Mary's ravaged face.

"Hi, Mum," was all she could manage to say, and that in a feeble whisper.

"I'm going to get another drink," Tin said tactfully and stood up. "I'll be up at the bar so you two can have a few moments. Mary, your usual?"

"Yeah, thanks, love." Mary's voice had a new hoarseness to it that Kate didn't remember from before.

Once Tin had walked away, the silence between the two women grew again. Kate, morbidly fascinated, couldn't stop herself from staring at Mary. Five years with not a hint of contact from her mother, not a call or a letter or a text, nothing... and then this shock meeting. Kate's thoughts flew to Magda and for a moment she wondered wildly about getting an emergency appointment, before bringing herself back to reality.

"Hello, Kelly," said Mary, eventually. She held her handbag on her lap like a shield, and her thin fingers fumbled inside it for what Kate guessed was a pack of cigarettes.

"You know you can't smoke in here," she said. Her voice sounded angry, more hostile than she intended and she saw Mary flinch.

"I've given up," said her mother.

Kate's eyes bulged. "You've *what*? Since when?"

Mary looked away. "Few months now."

Kate sat back in her seat, a little winded. Her mother had smoked like a chimney since before

Kate was born. Seeing Mary Redman without a cigarette in hand was incongruous, as if she were half-dressed or something equally ridiculous.

"Well, congratulations," said Kate and cringed inwardly at the jeer she could hear in her voice. What was wrong with her? Everything was coming out wrong.

Tin's hand appeared before Mary, holding a glass with what looked like a triple whisky.

"Here you go, Mary." Mary took it from him, looking up at him with a shaky smile. "What about you, Kate? Another lemonade?"

"No, I'd like a gin," said Kate, surprising herself. "A large gin with very little tonic. Please."

"Okay. Coming right up."

In any other situation, Kate would have felt a bit embarrassed about demanding an expensive drink just like that from a comparative stranger. As of now, though, she didn't care. Underneath the shock, she was beginning to feel the first stirrings of anger towards Tin Johnson and his surprises. She shoved those feelings back down and faced the more immediate emotions that facing her mother across the table engendered.

"So, how are you, Kelly?" asked Mary.

"It's Kate," Kate said automatically.

Mary dropped her gaze and said, "Oh yes, sorry. I keep forgetting."

Kate's eyes narrowed. Her mother had never

accepted her name change, way back in her teens, and had continued to call her Kelly whenever she could. Why had that changed? Briefly Kate thought back to being Kelly Redman. How long ago it seemed now. Why, she was a totally different person.

Tin came back to the table with Kate's drink, a tall glass packed with ice, tonic and a throat-flaming amount of gin. Kate took a deep swallow, fought not to do the 'drinking spirits face' that she always did, and put the glass back down on the table with something that was almost a bang. She could feel the gin making its way to her stomach in a long, burning trail.

"What's going on?" she asked, emboldened.

"What d'you mean?"

"Oh, come on, Mum." The word was out again and the two of them waited to see how the other would react.

Mary coughed again, harshly, the spasms shaking her thin body. After a few minutes, she sat back, wheezing and looked at Kate through watering eyes. "Nothing's going on. I don't know what you mean."

"What are you doing here?" Kate had to fight quite hard against the unexpected pity that was welling up inside her. Her mother looked so frail and vulnerable. She looked so *old*. Her hair was an unnatural coppery colour and hung in harsh strands around her thin face. It didn't look like her real hair. In fact, nothing about this woman looked like the mother Kate remembered at all. She had to stamp down on a sudden sense of paranoia that in fact this wasn't Mary Redman, that the woman was an imposter brought here to meet her for unknown purposes. Kate told herself not to be so ridiculous and took another large swallow of gin.

"I wanted to see you. I tried to call you but you didn't call me back..." Her mother was fighting back another cough. Kate waited impatiently for the coughing fit to end, but once her mother could draw breath again, it seemed as though she had run out of things to say.

"I saw your number. I didn't call you back because—" It was Kate's turn to pause. Why hadn't she rung back? "I didn't know whether you'd meant to do it or not. It's not like I'd heard from you lately. For Christ's sake, Mum, you're the one who told me to get lost, remember?" Kate was crouched forward now, talking in a furious, hissing whisper. "You told *me* to fuck off, remember? Slipped your mind, had it?"

Mary, who had normally been so quick to anger, now seemed to shrink beneath Kate's angry onslaught. She was shaking her head. "I was wrong to say that. Don't you think I don't know that, Kelly? All these years I wanted to see you, I wanted to say sorry, but I don't know – I just couldn't make that first step." Her voice was shaking now, the hoarseness gathering. Kate could see her fighting off another cough. "I just wanted to see you to say sorry."

"Fine," said Kate, some small mean part of her unable to forgive that quickly. "So why now? What's changed?"

Mary coughed, brought her thin, shaking hands to her mouth, coughed again. Kate could see her forcing herself to breathe normally by sheer effort of will. Mary looked up at her with streaming eyes. "I wanted to see you before it was too late."

Kate felt her heart beat suddenly, beat in thuds that she could feel throughout her ribcage. "What do you mean, before it's too late?" she asked, through numb lips.

"I mean I'm dying," said Mary Redman. "And I wanted to see you, to say sorry, before it was too late."

Chapter Six

"You all right?"

Kate looked up at the sound of Olbeck's voice. "What's that?"

Olbeck sat down on the corner of her desk. "Are you all right?" he repeated in the loud, slow voice of someone talking to an idiot.

Kate pulled herself together. "I'm fine," she said impatiently. She wasn't, of course; she was a long way from being *fine*, but there was no way she was going to discuss everything with Olbeck in the middle of a busy office. "Just thinking about things."

"God help us," said Olbeck, getting up. "You don't want to start *thinking*. Where would we be then?"

He winked at her and moved away, towards his office. Kate forced a smile and then turned back to her computer. Immediately, her thoughts reverted to her mother and the conversation they'd had in The Black Cat last night. Conversation was a misnomer. Kate had sat in frozen, silent horror whilst her mother had falteringly described her diagnosis, the treatment, the treatment she'd had after the first treatment had failed, the consultant's gentle but relentless prognosis – *he said six months, maybe longer if the chemo keeps working* – the pain, the sickness, the increasing frailty, the breathlessness, the fear...

Eventually, when Kate could bear it no longer, she managed to say "Okay, Mum, please stop. Please just let me—" and then her voice had failed her and she clamped her lips together, blinking hard. Taking in deep breaths, determined not to break down.

"I know it's a lot to take in," Mary had said, in her new, humble voice, and that had almost pushed her over the edge.

Tin had clearly noticed the jagged emotional tension emanating from their table and after a few minutes, he'd walked back to them, looking anxiously from one face to another.

"Everything all right?" he'd asked, tentatively.

Kate had welcomed the enormous surge of anger she'd then felt. Displacement, she knew that, but it had meant she didn't dissolve into a sobbing heap in public. She'd shot him a glance of fury that had made him step back a little and then turned to her mother who was sitting, still clasping her handbag as if its gaudy leather would protect her from anything that might assail her.

"Mum, I have to go now," Kate had managed to say, as gently as she could. "I'm not running away—" A lie and they both knew it. "I just need a bit of time... I'll call you tomorrow or in a couple of days. That's a promise. Or you can call me. But we'll speak again – we'll see each other again very soon. I promise."

She'd almost run to the door of the bar. Tin Johnson had clearly thought better about following her, proving he was quite intelligent after all. Kate, in the bustling office at the police station, didn't like to think about the ten minutes that followed, once she'd reached the comparative safety and privacy of her car. She looked down at her hands, probing at the tenderness along the sides of both with a wince. Her steering wheel wasn't designed to be pounded hard with clenched fists.

Kate sighed from the depths of her being. She'd checked her phone several times already that hour, but she found herself digging back into her handbag, bringing out her mobile. Three missed calls from Tin Johnson and two voicemails. A text from him too. *Please, Kate, could you give me a ring? I just want to be sure you're okay.* The *nerve* of the man... Nothing from Mary. Kate sighed again and put the phone back in her bag.

She squared her shoulders and straightened up from her slumped position. Aware that Rav was waving at her from across the room, Kate made her way over to his desk. "What's up?"

Rav looked pleased. He, at least, was looking a little more robust – his physiotherapy was obviously working. "I've heard from CAHID. They've got a definite date on the bones."

"Really?" asked Kate, feeling a welcome surge of excitement. Something to take her mind off everything else. "That's excellent. So what year are we talking?"

Rav paused dramatically. "Are you sure you're ready for this?"

"Yes," Kate said. "Don't drag it out."

Rav exhaled. "Nineteen seventy three."

"Seriously?" Kate was impressed and somewhat aghast. "That long ago? Jesus."

"I know. I wasn't even born then."

"Me neither."

They both looked at one another. Kate sat down on the edge of Rav's desk. "Blimey, this could be a bit more complicated than I thought. Did CAHID give you anything else?"

"Oh, yeah, of course. Got the whole report here."

He handed her a cardboard folder. "Thanks," Kate said. "Mind if I give it a quick once-over?"

"Be my guest. I'm off to update the boss."

Kate almost ran back to her own desk and opened the folder. As she began to read it, she marvelled at the scientific techniques that now allowed such a long ago crime to be investigated. Was it a crime

ECHO

though? Of course it was, she told herself. Bodies didn't bury themselves.

She read on. The bones belonged to a young woman, probably between sixteen and twenty one years of age. The centre had been thorough in their investigation. The woman had been Caucasian, her height estimated at between five foot two and five foot five, her weight approximately eight stone. The right humerus revealed an old fracture, probably sustained when she was a child, and she'd had two wisdom teeth removed. Kate re-read that paragraph. That could be really useful when checked against dental records. She made a few notes. What about DNA? They could check for matches against the National DNA Database. What about also checking for partial or familial matches? Kate scribbled her thoughts down as they occurred to her.

Intent on her work, she eventually sat back, easing the ache in her neck and back. For a blissful hour she hadn't thought about her mother – or Tin bloody Johnson – once, but, of course, the moment she relaxed, it all came flooding back. Kate jumped up, gritting her teeth, and made herself go and drink a glass of water before sitting back down again. As she did, she saw Theo walking across the office, past the window that faced the high street. She saw him glance casually out of the window, do a double take, and then stop and look. He started laughing.

Jane, who sat near the window, looked up at the sound. "What's up?"

"There's a bloke outside holding up a sign," said Theo, still chuckling. "What's he playing at?"

By now, everyone was looking. Kate began to get up.

"Look," said Theo, pointing him out to Fliss and Jane, who'd joined him at the window. "That black bloke there, with a sign saying 'sorry'."

Kate shot up from her seat and hurried across to the window. Surely not... But yes, there he was, Tin Johnson, holding up a hand-lettered sign and wearing an apologetic grin.

Kate made a strangled noise. The others looked at her.

"Don't tell me he's something to do with you," said Theo. His smile grew wider and more mischievous. "You're *joking*. Kate, what's he done? Kate?"

But Kate had already left the room at a run. She thundered down the stairs, out through the station reception, and hurried down the steps to the pavement.

"What are you playing at?" she hissed at Tin. She was conscious of a chorus of muffled cheering coming from the office window above her.

"Well, you wouldn't answer my calls," said Tin. He handed her the piece of paper with 'sorry' written on it. "So you forced me to take direct action. Here you go."

Kate took it, crumpled it into a ball and threw it on the ground. Then, because not even in extreme anger was she able to drop litter, she stooped and picked it up again. "I do not *believe* you." She began to walk quickly away. "Come on!" she threw back over her shoulder at Tin, who jumped and then hurried to keep up with her. She waved an extended middle finger in the vague direction of the crowd at the office window.

Once they were out of sight of the station, Kate came to a sudden halt and whirled around, hands on hips. "You're sorry? Really?" She put her hands up to the side of her head in a gesture of resignation and then dropped them. "You really thought it would be a wonderful idea to spring my dying mother on me?" Angry tears came to her eyes and she turned away, folding her arms.

Tin had stopped smiling. "I really am sorry," he said quietly. "I had Mary asking me to do it, and I didn't – I didn't know how to refuse her. Like you said, she's dying." Kate flinched and he went to put a hand out to her before drawing it back. "I'm sorry. I shouldn't have made it such a surprise. No wonder you got upset."

"Yes," Kate said, not trusting herself to say any more. Her throat was aching.

There was a moment's silence. Then Tin asked, still in that same quiet voice, "Are you going to call her?"

"That's none of your business," Kate said. Then she relented, a little. "I will talk to her. In my own time, and when I'm good and ready."

"All right," Tin said. "You're right, it's none of my business really. But – don't leave it too long. Please. She doesn't – Mary doesn't really have much time left."

Kate felt the tears brim over and swiped angrily at her face. She was still turned away from Tin but after a moment, his hand appeared in her peripheral vision, holding a clean tissue. She took it with a muttered thanks.

"Listen," said Tin. "You're right to be angry with me. I want to make it up to you. Can I buy you dinner?"

"I don't know," said Kate, snippily. "Can you?" She took refuge in sarcasm when upset, it wasn't one of her best traits but right at this moment, she didn't care.

Tin smiled sheepishly. "All right, Miss Pedant. *May* I buy you dinner?"

Kate sighed. She suddenly felt very tired. "Okay."

"Tonight?"

"I've got to work."

"Tomorrow?"

Kate considered refusing again. Why make it easy for him? But she was conscious that, despite her anger and upset, quite a big part of her really did want to have dinner with Tin Johnson. "Okay," she said in a tone that she purposefully made slightly more bored than she felt.

"Shall I pick you up from the station?"

"No. Just tell me where to go and I'll meet you there. And now, if you'll excuse me, I have to get back to work." With that, she turned smartly on her heel and walked away without a backward glance. She felt a twinge of anxiety as she turned the corner. Had she been a bit harsh? Too late now, if she had. Kate walked back up the steps to the station entrance, bracing herself for the storm of questions and teasing that was about to engulf her.

Chapter Seven

"I'LL GIVE YOU THIS," SAID Kate as she sat down in the restaurant Tin had chosen and looked about her. "You don't half know some nice places to eat."

"Well, I try," Tin said modestly. "It all stems from my days of having expense accounts. Sadly gone."

"But I bet that knowledge still comes in handy."

"It doesn't hurt," said Tin.

"Wine and dine a lot, do you?" asked Kate ironically.

"Oh yes. I'm out with a different woman every night, me. 'Shagger Johnson' is what they call me." He caught Kate's eye and laughed. "Oh, come on. What will you have to drink while we're waiting to order?"

Kate relaxed back into her chair as Tin went to fetch the drinks. Looking around the room, she was reminded of being out with Andrew – he'd had a penchant for fine dining but to be honest, this nice little bistro was probably a little too casual for him. Andrew had liked white linen tablecloths and hovering, deferential waiters, and Kate – well – hadn't. She liked places like this, where you could relax and enjoy the food without worrying about which fork you were supposed to use.

"I called my mother," Kate said as Tin sat down at the table again. She surprised herself – she hadn't meant to say that. Was she hoping for Tin's approval or something?

He raised his eyebrows. "That's good."

"I didn't actually get through. But I left her a voicemail." Kate wondered why she was continuing with this. "Anyway, not that it matters…"

The waiter approached their table and there was a necessary lull in conversation as they placed their orders. When the waiter had left, Tin leaned forward a little. "I was really glad you took me up on my offer. I wouldn't have blamed you if you hadn't."

"Well, that's very gentlemanly of you," said Kate, sarcasm dripping from every word. "I mean, why on Earth would I have been upset to have suddenly been confronted with a parent I'd been estranged from for half a decade?"

Tim looked sheepish. "How many times am I going to have to say I'm sorry? This isn't the best start to a new relationship, is it?"

Kate looked at him, startled. He didn't exactly blush, or if he did it wasn't apparent because of the tone of his skin, but there was an air of embarrassment about him, as if he'd suddenly been caught out in something he hadn't quite meant to say.

Kate wavered. Half of her wanted to take him up on the phrase 'new relationship', probably with an added side extra of sarcasm to boot. Half of her wanted to pretend he hadn't said it. She dropped her eyes to her menu, running her gaze over the printed dishes without seeing them.

The waiter brought their food and the moment itself fell away. They both chatted fairly easily about other things for a while: the weather, the various items of news that were currently hitting the headlines, their plans for the week ahead. Kate was surprised at how easy it was to talk naturally to Tin – after all, she barely knew him.

After their main course plates were cleared away, they both sat back a little, full of food and more relaxed than perhaps they had been at the start of the meal.

"So what made you become a cop?" Tin asked.

"'Cop'?" Kate tutted. "This isn't America, you know."

Tin's grin grew wider. "So, why you Babylon, innit?" Kate almost choked. "That any better?"

Kate laughed, despite herself. "That only proves you are definitely not down with the kids, Tin. *Babylon*. No one has said that since the nineteen eighties."

She liked the sound of his name, it sounded

natural and easy. Perhaps the same thought had occurred to him because he just chuckled at her admonishment and said "Tell me about it. I'm almost forty."

Kate raised her eyebrows. He looked a good ten years younger than that. "When's the big day?"

"April the seventeenth. Why? Will you come to the party?"

"If I'm invited," Kate said demurely.

"Oh, I think that's a given," Tin said. "Anyway, you're prevaricating. Why did you become a police officer?"

Kate dropped her gaze to the table, to the half empty wine glass which gave off a subdued sparkle in the candlelight. She'd been meaning to answer him in the same half-jokey fashion with which she'd been parrying most of his questions. Now, she didn't want to do that. She wanted to take him seriously and for Tin to take her seriously too.

"I wanted...order," she said slowly. "I wanted rules. I spent my childhood in utter chaos – there were no rules, or if there were, they weren't ever... enforced. I wanted – God, I just wanted the world to be...tidy."

Tin nodded as if he understood.

"How much have you talked to my mother?" Kate demanded. "What's she said about it? About what it was like bringing us up on her own?"

Tin shrugged. "She gave me the impression that

it was pretty hard work. She told me she'd already had two children taken into care when she was pretty young."

Kate nodded. "Terry and Manda. My older brother and sister. I never knew them."

"You don't see them now?"

Kate's gaze dropped to her wineglass once more. "Terry died when he was eighteen – a motorbike accident. I think Manda lives up north, somewhere. I think she's married, had a couple of children, but I don't ever see her. She probably barely knows I exist. They were both fostered from quite a young age, I think." She was silent for a moment and added, "Mum couldn't cope." The bitterness in her voice surprised her and she tacked on another sentence. "She couldn't cope with much, ever."

The warm and friendly atmosphere that had once existed between her and Tin seemed to have evaporated. Kate wondered whether he was condemning her for her hard words. What exactly had Mary told him?

"You probably think I'm very judgemental," she said, after a silence that seemed to grow too deep for comfort.

Tin shook his head. "You know what I think? I think you are but the person you judge the most, that you judge the hardest, is yourself."

Kate stared at him. To her horror, she felt tears begin to sting her eyes and looked away sharply, blinking hard. What a strange evening this was turning out to be – and there she'd been at home, getting ready, with Merlin twining around her ankles, thinking that she was going to enjoy it, that it was simply ages since she'd been on a date.

"Are you okay?" Tin asked, still in that warm and sympathetic voice. Perversely, she disliked him for it then – she didn't want him to pity her, she wanted him to admire her.

"I'm fine." She picked up her wineglass and emptied in it three swallows. "I hope you don't mind but I really do have to go now. I've got a very early start in the morning."

It was there, just for a flash – the look of disappointment. Kate didn't know whether she was sorry or glad. She didn't say anything but sat waiting for him to say something in return.

"Okay," Tin said eventually. "Can I give you a lift back?"

"No, I'll get a taxi," said Kate. She could hear the coldness in her voice and felt a horrid jab of despair, anger and frustration. It was all going wrong and she was making things worse. "Thank you for dinner," she said limply and Tin laughed, not very cheerfully.

"I'd be happier if I thought you'd actually enjoyed it," he said.

They both paused by the entrance to the restaurant. Kate pulled on her coat and felt another surge of those uncomfortable feelings at the bleak tone of his voice. Why did I ever think that this was a good idea? She asked herself, catching sight of her unhappy, taut face in the mirror that hung by the wall by the door.

On impulse she put a hand on his arm and the warmth beneath her palm seemed to melt away the anger and hostility that she was inexplicably feeling. "Tin," she said, and at last her voice had lost that hard edge. "I'm really sorry. I'm feeling – I'm all mixed up and I seem to be taking that out on you. I don't know why. I'm really sorry."

They stood very close together. Tin's face moved a little closer to Kate's and she thought, with a leap of the heart, that he was about to kiss her. He didn't though, but he put a finger to her mouth and then took it away.

"You don't have to apologise for anything," he said, very softly. "I just – if I can help, you only have to let me know."

Kate's mouth felt as if it were on fire, just from that gentle touch. She was lost for words for a moment and could only nod, dumbly. Then Tin stepped back a little and the charge between them dissipated.

"I'll buy dinner next time," said Kate. "If there is a next time."

"I'd like there to be," said Tin. "Just let me know."

Kate nodded. Then she said goodbye and turned

and left. She walked away down the street towards the taxi rank and didn't look back, but she was conscious of Tin watching her as she walked away, and suddenly she felt happy.

Chapter Eight

"So, Kate, how have you been?"

Magda always opened their counselling sessions with those words and Kate always replied in the same way. "Oh, I'm fine." Then she would reflect on how she was really feeling and go on to qualify her statement, just as she did today. "Actually, it's been a bit of a stressful week."

"Why don't you tell me about it?"

So Kate did, relaxing back into the green velvet sofa that her back and bottom had come to know intimately over the past few months. Kate had decided to seek some counselling last year, having been horrified by some of her behaviour – most notably to Olbeck during a very stressful case. She had cringed at the thought of talking to a perfect stranger about her problems but once she'd met Magda, and begun her treatment, she could feel it doing her good. She felt smoothed out, all those tangled threads and rough edges gradually beginning to unravel. She and Magda had worked their way through her childhood, through the events of her teens that had caused her so much anguish, right through her career as a police officer, her romantic attachments, the problems and regrets and mistakes that made up much of her life. And Kate, as she gradually untangled her emotions and feelings and decisions, found that she was being easier on herself. She had always taken pride in her work but she now found she could take pride in something else too – being strong enough to face up to where she'd gone wrong in the past and to take those lessons with her, into the future.

Tin's words from the dinner the previous night recurred to her as she talked to Magda. *The person you judge the most, that you judge the hardest, is yourself.* He was right, she realised. Perceptive guy. She found herself wondering when she could introduce him to Olbeck, to see what her best friend thought of him. She shook herself internally, bringing her focus back to the room and to what Magda was saying to her.

"So, how do you feel about re-establishing a relationship with your mother?" Magda asked.

Kate shrugged. "I'm not sure how I feel about it, to be honest."

"Well, that's understandable. Can you elaborate on your feelings? What's the uppermost one, the dominant emotion?"

Kate sat up a little. "You know, I hate to say it, but it's – it's anger. I actually feel furious at her.

79

Seriously, I could call her up right now and scream at her. That's awful, isn't it?"

Magda shook her head. "I'd say that was completely normal. You've not only got a huge amount of unresolved tension between you, not to mention your history, but anger can be a very normal reaction to news that someone is terminally ill. Death is such a big thing to confront that your mind almost wants to deflect it. You become angry at the person because you don't want to have to think about what's going to happen to them."

"Yes," Kate said. "I suppose so."

"If your mother were here now, and you could express how you were feeling towards her, what would you say?"

Kate shrank back against the chair. "No, I don't want to."

"It might help."

"No. No, I really don't want to."

Magda hesitated for a moment and then said, "That's up to you, Kate, of course. But I'd be cautious about repressing what you're feeling. You know we've talked about that before. You can't keep it down forever."

Kate sighed. "I know."

"Why not give it a try?"

Kate wavered, torn between knowing the truth of Magda's words and between feeling stripped raw, emotionally vulnerable. "Okay," she said eventually, reluctantly.

"Fine. Just imagine your mother is sitting across from you and just let yourself talk to her, naturally. Close your eyes if it helps."

Kate did so. She began to speak, feeling ridiculous. "Mum...hi, Mum. I wanted to talk to you the other day at the restaurant but I couldn't trust myself. I just couldn't believe that was you, after so many years. And I wanted to ask why it took you dying to come and find me." She stopped speaking for a moment, feeling the ache building in her jaw. "Why did you leave it so late? And you haven't said sorry, not once, not once for being such a shit mum all those years. And now you want my forgiveness? Just so you can die happy? Well, tough because it's too little, too late. I don't think you even care about me and how I'm feeling at all." Her voice broke then and she put one hand up to her mouth, her fingers trembling.

After a moment, Magda prompted her gently. "Did you want to carry on, Kate?"

Kate shook her head, unable to speak for a moment. After a few minutes, she put her hand down from her mouth and said hoarsely, "I don't want to do this anymore."

"All right," Magda said, just as gently. "We can leave it there if you want."

Later, as Kate closed the door of Magda's house behind her and walked down the four steps that led to the garden gate and the pavement beyond, she could still feel that tightness in her jaw. She understood what Magda was trying to do, and with the logical side of her mind, Kate could see the point. Therapy had taught her that the most painful things to confront were often the things that could make the biggest difference, if addressed. Kate knew all that – but she still didn't like it. She reached her car and unlocked it. She turned the heating up to full – somehow, she was always cold when she'd had a session with Magda. The blow of warm air on her face and hands was very comforting. She always sat for a moment, collecting herself, before trusting herself to drive.

By the time she arrived back at the station, Kate felt much more in control of herself. She had to spend the afternoon running data through various databases in an attempt to find a match with the information that the CAHID report had given them. She raised a hand to Olbeck as she walked in and saw him beckoning.

"What's up?" Kate asked, leaning on the doorframe of his office.

"Nothing work-related. Just wanted to know how your speech is coming along?"

"Sorry?" asked Kate, nonplussed. Then she realised. "Oh, um, it's fine. I haven't finished it yet."

"No worries – it's just that we've got the rehearsal

coming up in a fortnight and you'll need to have done it by then."

"I'll do it," said Kate, slightly annoyed. "You're turning into a right Bridezilla, did you know that?"

"Am I?" said Olbeck, shocked. "I'm not, am I?"

Kate relented. "No, not really. I guess you only get married once, you want it to be just right."

"I *hope* it's only once." Olbeck pushed his chair back from his desk and got up. "Anyway, moving on. Any further on an ID for our young woman?"

Kate and he walked back to Kate's desk, discussing the CAHID report. "I've asked to have it run through the DNA database, see if there's a match, obviously, but also if there's a partial match," Kate said.

"Good idea. God, the time lag makes such a difference. Nineteen seventy three – what are the chances of routine DNA collection then? Did that even happen?"

Kate shrugged. "Don't ask me."

Fliss leapt up. "I could find out. Do some research?"

Olbeck smiled at her. "That would actually be helpful, thanks, Fliss." He flicked the pages of the report back and forth. "Anyone got any other ideas?"

"Cold cases," said Theo, leaning back in his chair. "I thought of this last night. Why don't we cross check against the cold cases from that sort of era, see if there's anything that comes up? I mean, our vic's young, female – she might be a forgotten victim of a serial killer, or something like that."

"Yep," Olbeck said absently, head bent to the report again. "Another good idea."

Fliss had been busy typing at her computer. "The first conviction involving DNA profiling was in nineteen eighty six," she said, reading aloud from the screen.

"Right," said Olbeck. "Well, that helps. Has anyone checked the dental records yet?"

"Waiting to hear back," Rav said, smartly. "Although again, the time lapse might mean we get nothing. Do dentists normally keep records for forty years?"

As one, they turned to Fliss who smiled and reiterated her previous remark. "Leave it with me," she finished.

After that, they all separated, moving back to their individual desks. Kate pushed up her sleeves, pulled her chair in tight to her desk, and turned to her computer screen, determined to track down the young woman in the missing persons database. Wouldn't it be great, she thought, if I get a match straight away? But as she tapped keys and read, she had an inkling that it wouldn't be that straightforward.

It wasn't. After several hours of searching, Kate knew that there was nothing to be found. She'd expected it, but it was still frustrating. She sat back, easing the ache in her shoulders from where she'd been sitting hunched forward – a very bad idea, she reminded herself; she really should have known better. She got up and stretched, looking over to where Theo was doing what she'd just chastised herself for.

"Oi, straighten up, Theo," she called over. "Remember your posture."

Theo looked at her, startled. "What?"

"Oh, never mind." Kate wandered over to his desk and perched on the edge of it. "Guess what?"

"What?"

"There's no missing persons match."

Theo's face flickered for a moment, then cleared. "Well, I can't say I'm surprised. What about DNA?"

Kate shook her head. "Nothing's come back. However, I might just have one more trick up my sleeve."

"Oh yeah?"

Kate pushed herself upright. "I read up on it last night. There was a case – funnily enough in 1973 – where three young girls were raped and strangled in South Wales."

Theo grimaced. "Nice."

"Well, eventually – years and years later, in the noughties, I think - someone did develop a DNA profile from the crime scene samples. Enough to run through the national database."

Theo raised an eyebrow. "And they found a match?"

Kate shook her head. "Nope. No match. But about a year later, the investigating officer decided to search for partial matches – basically looking for a family connection. And guess what? He found one. Some car thief had had a DNA swab and that was a fifty percent match to the crime scene DNA. And that's how they tracked the killer down."

Theo nodded. "And you're telling me this rather than searching the records because…?"

Kate grinned. "I just wanted to tell you because it makes me sound rather clever to have thought of it, don't you think?"

Theo snorted. "Makes you sound like a nutter, more like. Come back and tell me when you've actually found something."

"Oh, Theo," Kate said, mock-sorrowfully. "You're no fun." She dodged the paperclip he threw at her with a giggle and went back to her desk.

Habit made her check her phone before she got back to work. The smile was wiped off her face when she saw she had a text from her brother, Jay. *What's up, sis? J x*. Kate had called him last night and left a voicemail that she needed to talk to him. Why hadn't he just called her back, rather than texting? Perhaps he couldn't talk, she told herself. It was the middle of a working day, after all. But what if he hadn't called her because he knew what it was she wanted to talk to him about, and he was actually avoiding her?

Such paranoia, Kate. She texted Jay back *Will call you again later x* and turned back to her work.

She got home that evening early enough to make that phone call possible. She drew out a portion of home-made lasagne from the freezer and popped it into the microwave to defrost and cook. One of the ways in which she was trying to be a bit nicer to herself, on Magda's advice, was to feed herself healthy, home-cooked food rather than relying on ready meals and takeaways. It had been hard at first – Kate got home so exhausted some nights that even heating a pizza up was beyond her – but she'd learned to plan ahead, make a big batch of freezable food and portion it up to eat at her leisure. As the microwave whirred, Kate keyed in Jay and Laura's home number and prepared herself.

Laura answered and Kate had a few minutes of pleasant small talk with her before she asked to speak to Jay. It could have been her imagination, but Kate thought that there was the slightest hesitation in Laura's voice as she answered "Of course, I'll go and get him. He's glued to the X-Box at the moment."

"Thanks," said Kate. She pressed the phone to her ear, trying to hear Jay and Laura's conversation but nothing could be heard except vague, low murmurs. Eventually Jay came onto the line.

"Hi, sis. How you doing?"

He sounded normal as ever, but was there just

a slight wariness, just a shade of constraint in his tone? Again, Kate told herself not to be paranoid.

They chatted about inconsequential things for a few minutes: work, the weather, Jay and Laura's upcoming holiday to Spain. Then Kate girded her loins. "Have you spoken to Mum, lately?"

There was a short silence although Kate could hear Jay's faint breathing on the other end of the line. "Why?" he asked, eventually.

"Come on," said Kate, an edge to her tone. "I think you know why. You know, don't you?"

There was another pause, and then Jay sighed. "Yeah. I know."

"Why didn't you tell me?" Kate burst out, louder than she'd intended to. She could hear a tremble in her voice.

"Kate, come on. I wanted to tell you, of course I did, but Mum told me not to. She said she wanted to see you herself, tell you herself. She totally *forbade* me to say anything. What was I supposed to do?"

Kate struggled against another burst of anger. She knew it was mainly against herself. Of course Jay couldn't have gone back on a promise to their mother. It was her news to tell. Kate knew that – but still... She swallowed hard, biting back the words she wanted to say but knew she'd regret if she did.

"You should have told me," was all she said limply, after a moment. Jay said nothing and the two of them breathed down the phone at each other for another minute or two.

"How are you feeling about it, anyway?" Jay asked quietly.

"I'm fine," Kate said, her automatic response to anything uncomfortable. She paused, remembered that this was her brother she was talking to, the relative she was closest to. "I'm a bit shocked, actually. A bit shaken. She just looked so – so *ill* when I saw her."

"Yeah. Poor Mum, she's not looking too clever."

Kate thought back to her mother sitting across the table from her, her thinness, the shadows on her face, the strange coppery hair that sat slightly wrongly on Mary's head. A wig, Kate only now realised. Of course it would be a wig, what with the chemotherapy and everything.

She steeled herself and asked him the question that she really wanted the answer to. "How long do you - do you think she's got?"

"I'm not sure," said Jay. His voice was almost steady. Kate suddenly had a vision, as clear as if she could see down the phone line: Laura sat close beside Jay on the sofa at their flat, while he talked to her, her hand on his arm, warmth and love in her touch. Kate closed her eyes briefly, conversely warmed and saddened by the sight. Thank God Jay has someone to care for him, had someone on his side. *But what about me?* Kate pushed the thought away with an effort.

"The hospital said six months to a year," Jay was saying. "But from what I've been reading and hearing about, that doesn't really mean anything. In fact, it could well be an overestimate."

Kate again closed her eyes briefly. She remembered Tin saying something similar to her, that afternoon in the park. *Don't leave it too long. Please. She doesn't – Mary doesn't really have much time left.* The jab of pain caught her unawares.

"You okay?" asked Jay.

"I'm fine." Kate straightened up and pushed her hair back from her face. She and Jay talked a little more, skirting around the edges of the conversation both of them were aware that they should be having, but neither of them quite able to breach the conversational gap. In the end, talk about Mary petered out and they were left to say their goodbyes.

"Let's catch up soon," said Kate, more sincerely. She missed her brother.

"Yes, we must. When we get back from Spain."

Once Kate had put the phone down, she stared ahead of herself for a moment. Then she brought Mary's number up on her mobile screen. Her thumb hovered above the 'call' icon, but she somehow wasn't able to bring herself to press it. Tomorrow, she promised herself. I'll call her tomorrow.

Chapter Nine

KATE WOKE THE NEXT MORNING to something that had almost become a novelty – bright sunshine. She pushed the bedroom window curtains aside and looked out onto a flawless morning, the sky a bright blue, the pavements dry. With delight, she noticed that the tree outside her house was finally budding. Eagerly, she got up and dressed and made breakfast for herself and Merlin, eating it standing by the back door and looking out onto the sunny garden. It was incredible how a bit of sun could make her feel a hundred times better.

Buoyed by the good weather, Kate grabbed her mobile phone and, without hesitating, rang her mother. She waited, listening, telling herself not to tense up. It was something of an anti-climax when the phone call went to voicemail. Kate pulled herself together and left a message for her mother in a tone that was as steady and as cheerful as she could make it, suggesting meeting for tea and cake at a time that would suit Mary Redman. She signed off by saying "Take care, Mum," and hung up, feeling that sense of relief that comes from finally tackling a much-hated job. Why had she procrastinated for so long when actually, when it came to it, the task wasn't so bad after all? Kate stroked Merlin on his black, glossy head in goodbye and headed out the front door.

Even the sight of the piles of paperwork on her desk didn't daunt her. Kate squared her shoulders and sat down, pulling her chair closer to her desk. After a moment, she realised Rav was waving at her across the room.

"What's up?" she asked, making her way over to him.

Rav looked excited. "We've got a DNA match."

Kate was conscious of a jab of annoyance, even under her exclamation of happy surprise. She'd wanted to be the one to find it – she'd worked so damn hard on sifting through all that data – but even she couldn't keep working through the night on it. She told herself it didn't matter. Surely the important thing was that they finally had a match.

"That's great," she said, leaning forward to look at Rav's computer screen. "That's brilliant. A full match?"

Rav shook his head. "Nope, not that good. Partial only, so it must be a family connection. Here, I've printed it out for you. I know you've been working really hard on this."

"Oh, thank you," said Kate, grateful that her efforts had at least been acknowledged by one person. She patted Rav on the arm affectionately and made her way back to her desk, clutching the sheaf of papers he'd given her.

The DNA profile from the bones had been partially matched to another profile on the database. Kate looked at the name and age. Kayla Tripp, aged twenty-five, arrested for assault. Kate read through the details, frowning. Could this Kayla be the daughter of the woman whose bones had been found? Kate did some quick mental arithmetic. If Kayla was twenty-five, then she would have been born in nineteen ninety. That meant it was impossible for her to be the daughter. So what was the connection?

Kate went back over to Rav's desk and told him what she thought.

"Yeah, I'd worked that out too," Rav said. "The dates don't match, not even close. But there must be a connection."

"A niece, perhaps. Can't be a sister, can it?"

"Nope. We should talk to her though, eh? This Kayla Tripp."

"Absolutely."

Rav and Kate both looked at the address details on the report sheet and groaned in unison.

"Sheffield! Bloody hell..." said Rav.

Kate smiled. "I'll drive."

"We can't get there and back in a day, surely?"

Kate pondered. "No, probably not. Besides, we might need to talk to other members of her family." She jumped up. "I'll just run it past Mark and we can get going."

Olbeck approved the trip, and Kate and Rav were soon in the car and on their way to the motorway. Kate tapped the steering wheel in time to the music, glad to be out of the office and finally doing something constructive. She said as much to Rav.

"God, I know. I was starting to think we were never going to get anywhere with this case."

"Me too." Kate adroitly steered the car into the inside lane. "Still, there's always *something*, isn't there. That's what Anderton says. You always get some sort of a break." She considered for a moment and added, "Not necessarily in time, though, it has to be said."

The traffic, for once, was quite light and reasonably fast moving. Kate and Rav made good time and found themselves on the outskirts of Sheffield by late afternoon. Kate, having not visited the city before, was thankful for her sat nav. The traffic gradually got heavier as the offices, schools and other places of work closed for the day and the rush hour began. It was an hour and forty minutes later when they finally drew into the crowded car park of the Holiday Inn where they would be staying for the next few days.

Rav had attempted, whilst en route, to contact Kayla Tripp but without success. He and Kate conferred in the reception area of the hotel once they'd checked in.

"We've got a last known address," said Kate. "That's got to be our first port of call. If not, there's another contact number here for her next of kin, her mother." She scanned the page again and frowned. "Maybe we should try her mother first, actually. After all, if it *is* a family connection, time-wise, it's more likely the mother might know more about it than a twenty-something."

Rav walked abruptly to a nearby seat and sat down. Kate looked at him sharply. "You all right?"

Rav had one hand to his stomach. "I'm all right," he said with an effort, after a moment. "Sitting for hours in the car with that seat belt against me wasn't that good."

Kate bit her lip. "Maybe you should go and rest. I can do this."

"No. I'm coming." Rav took a deep breath and struggled to his feet. "Otherwise what's the point of me being here?"

"Uh-huh." Kate put a hand on his shoulder and gently turned him around. "Go on, go and lie down for a bit. Did you bring your painkillers?"

"Yes."

"Well, take a couple, get some rest and I'll report back soon. Besides, you could try and track down some more of the Tripp family, see if there's anyone else around that we could talk to."

Rav wavered for a moment and then gave in. "Yeah, I guess I could do that."

"Want me to help you up to your room?"

"No," Rav said impatiently. "I'm fine. I'll just – lie down for a bit and start looking through some more data."

"Okay." Kate made herself step back a little and watched him make his slow and faltering way to the lifts. Rav had never been what you'd call robust, but since the incident and his recovery he'd grown so thin he was almost child-like in stature. Kate had to force herself not to go over and put her arms around him, helping him along. He wouldn't like that. She made herself give him a cheery smile and wave as the lift door shut and she caught his eye and he grinned in return, just before the closing doors cut him off from view. Kate dropped her hands to her sides and exhaled. Then she checked the report again to see where it was she had to go.

Despite the satellite navigation, Kate still got lost twice looking for Kayla Tripps's address. As she finally pulled into the side of the correct street, she heard the buzz of her mobile phone as a voicemail alert came through. She'd missed another call from her mother, but at least this time Mary had left a message. Kate listened, wincing inwardly at the hoarseness in her mother's voice. She sounded worse than she had the other night. Surely she sounded worse? Kate pressed the 'repeat message' button and listened again. Mary had agreed to meet her on Friday, in the tea room that Kate had suggested. Kate felt an absurd surge of panic at the thought of facing her mother again, despite the fact that she'd suggested it. She stamped down on the feeling, told herself that she was being ridiculous, and conjured Magda's calm and soothing tones in her head, thinking over all the times she and her therapist had discussed her mother. After a moment, she felt more in control. Even so, she didn't call her mother back but instead sent a text confirming the meeting on Friday. She dithered over ending the text with a kiss. She put one in and then deleted it again. Her mother's wasted face facing her over the table at The Black Cat came to mind again and Kate, shaking her head impatiently, added the kiss again to the end of her message and sent it.

She got out of the car, stretched and looked about her. Whittington Road was a nondescript street, lined end to end with small, terraced red brick houses, thrown up in their thousands, perhaps millions, during the Victorian and Edwardian eras. Kate could see little, brave touches here and there – a freshly painted door, a window box with some early daffodils – but the overall impression was of poverty and making-do and tiredness.

She found Kayla Tripp's last known address

and knocked at the house. Nobody answered. Kate knocked again, tried the (broken) doorbell, knocked and waited once more and then retreated to the car, wanting to get out of the cold wind. So, no luck with Kayla. The only contact number they had for her wasn't working or had been cut off. Kate looked at the only other name on the sheet, a Jackie Tripp, Kayla's mother. She keyed the address into her sat nav, turned the car around, with some difficulty in the narrow street, and set off to find her. It was worth a try at least.

As it turned out, Jackie Tripp lived in an almost identical house, in a very similar street, some two miles away. There were limp, yellowed net curtains at the windows that gave it a bleary, run-down look. Jackie Tripp had much the same look, Kate thought, as the door opened and a faded, middle-aged woman stood there, blinking in the light as if she'd just emerged from a dark tunnel.

"Jackie Tripp?"

"Yes," the woman said, looking at first puzzled and then apprehensive. Kate hastened to reassure her and explained why she was there. It was an explanation that necessarily took a little while, and even after she'd given it, Jackie Tripp stood looking at her with very little comprehension.

"You what, love? DNA sample?"

Kate patiently explained again, finishing by asking if she could come in for a minute. Jackie nodded, still obviously confused, but stepped back to allow Kate to step over the threshold.

It was a house where the front door led straight into the living room. It was a small room, cluttered with too much furniture. A large black cat lay curled in front of the gas fire. Kate thought for a fanciful moment that it could be Merlin's brother, it was so like him. A secondary thought occurred to her that she needed to text Olbeck, to see if he'd remembered to pop in and feed Merlin, as he'd promised.

"I've got a cat just like him," she said, pointing, hoping a little small talk would ease the look of worried confusion on Jackie Tripp's face.

Jackie said nothing in response but nodded, a little warily. "Sit down, love," said Jackie, indicating a sagging settee covered in magazines, tabloid newspapers, crumpled tissues and a pile of clean but unfolded washing.

Kate perched on the few clear inches towards the arm of the settee.

"I'm sorry, love, I don't quite understand what you're here for," said Jackie, once more. "It is something to do with our Kayla? Is she in trouble again?"

"No, it's nothing like that, Mrs Tripp. I appreciate it's quite confusing. I'm from Abbeyford CID, that's a town in the West Country, near Bristol?" Kate leant forward a little, hoping she wasn't going too fast. Jackie nodded tremulously. Kate went on to explain the discovery of the long-buried body, the fact that the DNA profile they'd been able to take had matched, in significant proportions, the DNA sample that had been taken from Kayla Tripp. She spoke as slowly and as clearly as she could, trying to keep the jargon to a minimum. "Is that clear to you now, Mrs Tripp? We believe that the body we found in Munford Gorge is in some way related to Kayla. I understand you're Kayla's mother?"

Jackie nodded at this, a little more emphatically as though that, at least, was something that she was sure of. Kate took a deep breath and went on. "That's very helpful to know, Mrs Tripp, because – and I hope this isn't too distressing for you – because that also means that the remains that we found recently are in some way related to you."

Jackie received this news in silence. Kate could see her digesting the information and braced herself for some sort of emotional outburst as the news sank in. But there was nothing, nothing except a faint expression of puzzlement on Jackie's worn face.

"Has there ever been anyone reported missing in your immediate or close family? Someone who may have gone missing as long ago as nineteen seventy-three?"

There was a flicker on Jackie's face and Kate sat forward a little. But then Jackie shook her head. "No. No, love, I can't think of anyone."

Kate sat back again. "No one at all? No one in the wider family?" she persisted.

Jackie Tripp was rubbing her hands together nervously. "I can't think – I don't think so."

Tamping down her frustration, Kate tried to think of the best way to frame her next question. She was beginning to doubt herself. Could the DNA be wrong? Had there been some cross-contamination somewhere? It did happen. If that was the case, then she was wasting her and Jackie Tripp's time.

"Is there anyone in the family that you haven't heard from for a long time?"

Jackie's face flickered again. Kate could see her beginning to shake her head and her lips to frame another negative sentence. Then she stopped.

"There was me sister, Jean," said Jackie. "I haven't heard from her in years. But she went abroad, love. She sent me postcards."

Kate sat forward again. "Your sister? Kayla's aunt?"

"Yes. But it can't be *her*. She went to Spain."

Kate took a deep breath. "Can you remember exactly when you last saw Jean, Mrs Tripp?"

Jackie's nervous hands continued to rub together as she thought. "Oh, it were years ago. She was older than me. Always a bit wild. Ended up going down to London, thought she was going to be one of those models. She was pretty, though, I'll give her that. Maybe she did end up being a model."

Kate controlled her impatience. "When did Jean go to London, Mrs Tripp?"

"Oh, I can't remember exactly. How old was I? Ten, I think. Jean was older, five years older, so she would have been fifteen. So when would that have been?" She paused, clearly calculating in her head. "It's funny, love, but I think that *would* have been the early seventies. Maybe nineteen seventy-two. God, it seems so long ago now..." Her voice drifted off and Kate waited until it became clear that Jackie wasn't going to say anything more.

"Mrs Tripp, you've been really helpful, but I just need to clarify a few things. You had a sister, an older sister called Jean, who left for London at the age of fifteen? And you think this was in the early nineteen seventies?" Mrs Tripp nodded. "And you haven't heard from her since?"

"No, no that's not right," Jackie said emphatically. "She sent us postcards, at least two postcards from Spain. Said she was living there. I remember, because I got quite excited at the thought of visiting her. I'd never been to Spain. Never been abroad, then."

"Do you still have the postcards, Mrs Tripp?"

Jackie laughed nervously. "Somewhere, love, but look around you." She gestured at the mess and clutter. "It would take me all day to find them."

Kate nodded in understanding. Long experience had taught her that it was no use offering your help in the search. "Can you tell me if the postcards were in your sister's writing? Or were they typed?"

Jackie looked confused once more. "I can't remember, love. It were so long ago. I just remember Mum telling us we had a postcard from our Jean one morning. Maybe it was only the one that came."

"It would be really helpful for our investigation if you could find those cards, or that card if there was only one. Not now, I don't mean that, but if you could have a look over the next day or so and give me a call." Kate handed over her own business card. "Do you know if a missing persons report was ever filed for Jean? Did your mother ever report her missing, that you know of?"

Mrs Tripp took the card nervously from Kate and held it carefully in both hands. She was shaking her head. "She was never missing, she just left home. She didn't come back again but she weren't *missing*."

Kate tamped down the feeling of impatience that these answers were inducing. She wondered how she could tactfully ascertain whether Mrs Tripp's mother was still alive and able to be questioned. "So, as far as you know, Jean was never reported missing?"

"No. She wasn't."

Kate took the bull by the horns. "Would it be possible for me to speak to your mother directly, Mrs Tripp?"

"She died last year."

Kate had been expecting something of the kind, but she nodded and murmured something sympathetic. Quickly she glanced down at her notes, wondering if she'd missed anything. Oh yes, there was that...

"I'm sorry if this sounds like a strange question, but would you remember if Jean ever broke her arm as a child?"

Jackie Tripp was frowning. Kate had the impression that her confusion was now bordering on bewilderment and told herself to slow it down, take it easy. She was an experienced interviewer, after all; she should know how to reset the tone of the questions if it looked as though they were becoming distressing.

"Broke her arm? What do you mean? I don't know, I'm sure – I can't remember..." Jackie was finally beginning to look a little tearful.

Kate hastened to soothe her. "You've been very, very helpful, Mrs Tripp – I'm really so grateful. I know it's not always the easiest of things to undergo, particularly after such a long time."

Jackie blinked and managed a tremulous smile.

"There is one other thing you can do for me, which would really help," said Kate, rather hesitantly. "Would I be able to take a DNA sample from you? It's completely painless, it's just a mouth swab, that's all."

Jackie looked worried. "Oh, I don't know about that. What would it – would it—"

"It would be really helpful to us," said Kate quickly, talking over her. "We could then match it against the DNA we have already. I promise you it doesn't hurt – and we wouldn't store in the National Database or anything like that. It would just be for the purposes of this investigation."

Jackie acquiesced, rather hesitantly, and Kate took the swab and sealed it in an evidence bag. "Thank you so much, Mrs Tripp. That will be really useful."

As she said goodbye to the older woman at the door, Kate could feel and hear her mobile ringing in her pocket. She smiled a last goodbye at Jackie Tripp and turned away, striding down the street before answering the phone. It was Rav.

"God, I'm so sorry I haven't called before. I just woke up. Did you get anything?"

"Yes, and I'm on my way back. I think we might be able to get an ID but it depends on how quick I can get this sample to the labs." Kate explained where she had been, talking rather breathlessly as she walked quickly towards her parked car.

"I'll get the hotel to organise a courier," said Rav. "We can get that sample biked over and get the express turnaround."

"Fabulous. See you soon." Kate hung up, flung the mobile on the passenger seat along with the evidence bag and gunned the engine, impatient to get things started. As she drove away, the lowering grey clouds were pierced by a shaft of golden sunlight and she chose to interpret that as a good omen. It seemed they were finally making some headway after all.

Chapter Ten

THE NEXT AFTERNOON SAW RAV and Kate back at the Abbeyford station, after a long and tiring drive back from Sheffield that morning. Both were waiting impatiently for the call from the National DNA Database to confirm whether or not the sample from Jackie Tripp matched the DNA sample from the body. Kate kept looking towards her telephone, thinking perhaps if she willed it hard enough, the phone call might come through, forced into being by her mind. It didn't, of course. She kept jumping up to make cup after cup of coffee, each one abandoned to go cold after she'd drunk half.

When at last the telephone finally rang, Kate actually jumped. She was so eager to pick it up that she almost dropped the receiver in her haste to answer it. At first, she was almost disappointed to hear Jackie Tripp's tremulous voice on the other end of the line. "I've remembered, love, about Jean's arm. You asked me about it yesterday?"

Kate tamped down her impatience and

disappointment at the call not being from the laboratory. "Oh, yes, I remember."

Jackie went on, sounding a bit surer of herself. "Well, it's funny that I forgot about it but you know, love, Jean did actually break her arm when she was a kiddie. I remember because she let me draw a flower on the cast. I must have only been about eight. She came off her bike coming down the hill and went into someone's car door."

Kate sat up straighter at the leap of excitement. All right, so it wasn't definitive proof but it was another piece of the jigsaw puzzle. "That's so helpful, Mrs Tripp. Can you remember which arm it was that Jean broke?"

"Her right one. I remember because she couldn't do any school work for a month because she couldn't write. Not that Jean was ever much good at that sort of thing."

"That's brilliant." Kate scribbled down as much detail as she could. "Would you remember the name of your family doctor, Mrs Tripp, by any chance? I know it's – oh, Doctor Gregson, you say?" She wrote the name down. It might come in handy for comparing X-rays and medical notes. "Thank you so much for letting me know. I don't suppose you've been able to find that postcard that Jean sent to you?" She very nearly said 'supposedly sent to you' but managed to restrain herself. As it turned out,

Mrs Tripp hadn't found it. Kate thanked her anyway and said goodbye.

The phone rang almost immediately after she put the receiver down. Kate lunged for it again and this time it was the laboratory with the results of the DNA test. Kate listened to what they had to say, suppressed a whoop of joy, thanked them for their time and put the phone down. Then she ran across the room to Rav's desk and virtually threw herself on it.

"It's a match?" he said breathlessly. Kate nodded, grinning. Rav let out a shout of "Yes!" that turned heads across the office.

"Close familial match to the DNA from the bones. Closer than the match with Kayla Tripp. This is it, Rav. We have an ID."

Kate bounced back upright. Rav was beating his hand on the edge of his desk in a victory tattoo. "This is too cool for school," he said, his face alight. "We've only gone and bloody got an ID."

"I'll tell Mark and Anderton," said Kate. "Our victim is Jean Tripp, never reported missing."

"You know what this means?" asked Rav.

"What?"

"We'll have to go up to bloody Sheffield again."

Kate shook her head, grinning. "Don't care. We got a match!"

She bounded her way across the office to Olbeck's office. He'd been alerted already by Rav's shout and Kate's general demeanour.

"That's brilliant," he said once she informed him

of what they found. "Come with me and we'll tell Anderton together."

It was on the short walk to Anderton's office that Kate's elation began to cool. It was good, obviously, that they'd finally been able to identify the body but where exactly did that get them? If Jean Tripp had been missing for over forty years, what was the likelihood that they would be able to identify her killer? She hadn't even been reported missing by her family. If she had indeed gone to London, and met her killer there, how on Earth were Kate and the team going to be able to track him or her down?

"Oh, nil desperandum, Kate. Nil desperandum," Anderton said cheerfully as she unloaded her worries before him as she and Olbeck took seats at his desk. "Don't go looking for trouble, that's my motto."

"Yes, you thought we might not even be able to get an ID at one point, didn't you?" asked Olbeck. "But we did."

"Exactly, Mark," Anderton said. "So let's have no more of this pessimism. We're a gigantic step forward and we've just got to think of where we move to from here."

"I guess re-interviewing Jackie Tripps is a priority," Kate said. "Poor woman, we've got to break the news to her that her long-lost sister is dead."

"Well, perhaps the intervening years will soften the blow," Anderton said. "Kate, are you able to go back to Sheffield to do that tomorrow?"

Kate opened her mouth to say yes but realised that she'd already arranged to meet her mother the following evening. For a second, she thought about cancelling the arrangement and then realised that she wouldn't be able to. She couldn't prioritise work over her family, not this time, much as she wanted to.

She explained, reluctantly, why she couldn't go and Anderton, who knew something of her relationship with her mother but not of her mother's illness, nodded. "Theo and Rav can go," was his only comment.

Olbeck looked at Kate with some surprise. She realised she'd hardly had a chance to talk to him about anything recently: not about her mother, or Tin, or anything that wasn't to do with his and Jeff's upcoming nuptials. She felt a stab of guilt at the realisation that she hadn't even started writing her speech.

Anderton was still speaking. "We need to build a picture of Jean Tripp's whereabouts when she left Sheffield. Where did she go in London? Did she ever reach London? Kate, if you're office-bound, can you start doing some digging on her name, anything you can pull up – medical records, arrest records, even newspaper articles? Just see if you can find anything that will give us a clue as to where she might have ended up."

Kate nodded. The three of them spent some time discussing questions to be put to Jackie Tripp and other members of Jean Tripp's family up in Sheffield. Then, with a repetition from Anderton that they were not to lose hope on getting anywhere with this case, Olbeck and Kate made their way back to their office.

Kate worked as hard as her tired brain would allow her that afternoon. She made telephone calls, trawled through databases and scribbled notes but without making much progress. One thing she was able to track down were Jean Tripp's medical records, from her old doctor's surgery. The surgery, now a much bigger medical centre for that suburb of Sheffield, apparently had archives of their patients' medical records dating back to World War Two. Kate obtained a promise, from the clerk at the storage facility, that Jean Tripp's medical notes would be sent on by courier. She looked down at her list of things to do and made a large, bold tick against that item. One down, many more to go. She stretched and yawned, wondered about pushing on for another hour with the help of several strong coffees but rejected the idea. Merlin would need feeding and she desperately needed some sleep. Besides, she had to strengthen herself for the meeting with her mother tomorrow. *And* she had to write that bloody wedding speech. Kate sighed and got up, picking up her bag, and walked towards the exit, mentally writing and rewriting lists in her head.

Chapter Eleven

THE TEA ROOM WHERE KATE had arranged to meet her mother was one she frequented regularly. As she climbed the few steps to the front door of the café, Kate could see through the window that her mother was already there, seated with her back to the window. She had a moment's regret that she'd suggested this place. It was a place of happy memories, of afternoon teas with Olbeck and Jeff, of quiet mornings on her own, with a steaming pot of tea and a plate of scones, the Sunday newspaper on the table in front of her. Now, all that was probably going to be tainted.

Oh, stop being so melodramatic, Kate, she told herself and pushed open the door. She wasn't sure whether to kiss her mother or not, and they both settled for an awkward sort of half-hug. Kate sat down opposite Mary Redman. She looked worse than she had when Kate had first seen her at The Black Cat. She looked as though she were slowly fading away. Kate tried not to show her distress.

"How are you, love?" Mary asked, in a voice that was surely even hoarser than it had been two weeks before.

"I'm fine," said Kate, hastily. "And you?"

Mary shrugged. "About the same."

"Right." Their tea came and Kate busied herself with pouring cups, arranging cakes on plates, handing over a napkin. After the bustle of that, silence fell.

"Coppers treating you all right, are they?" Mary asked. She had always used to ask that, whenever she saw Kate, and Kate always answered in the same way, as she did now.

"Fine, thanks."

They both looked away and sipped their tea. A lengthier silence fell. Kate kept her eyes on the shimmering brown surface of her tea cup, thinking how excruciating this was.

"You spoke to Tin recently?" Mary said eventually.

Kate gave a non-committal nod. She didn't want to tell her mother that she'd arranged another dinner date with him for the following night.

"Handsome lad, in't he?" Mary had put down her cup and was dabbing the napkin around her mouth like a lady. "You could do a lot worse there, Kel – Kate."

"Yes, all right," said Kate, more testily than she'd meant to. "There's nothing like that going on." Well, she reasoned with herself, there wasn't at the moment. Despite herself, she felt a leap of excitement at the thought of what might happen tomorrow night. Aloud, she said, "I understand you've been talking to him about your experiences of the Marhaven care home." She noted with her police officer's eye the slight flinch that Mary gave at the mention of the home. "Is that right?"

Mary coughed and cleared her throat. It was Kate's turn to wince at the thick rattle of phlegm. Mary coughed, coughed again and wiped her mouth with the napkin. "Yeah, I've been talking to him," said Mary. "I want to set the record straight before I – before I go."

"What is there to tell?"

Mary looked at her with watering eyes. "There were bad things going on at the care home. People got away with stuff for far too long. Now it's time to put things right, as much as I can, while I still can."

Kate leant forward a little. "What kind of bad things?"

Mary dropped her eyes. She was quiet for a moment and then said, in a hoarse, low voice "Bad things. Girls given out to people, to men. It was a *care* home, there were girls there who were children. They were supposed to take care of us."

Kate was silent for a moment, thinking. "Are you saying this happened to you?"

"Sort of." Mary coughed again, wiped her mouth again with the sodden tissue.

"Let me get you a fresh one," said Kate, trying to hide her disgust. She delved in her bag for an unopened pack of tissues and gave it to her mother. "What do you mean, sort of?"

Mary slit the plastic of the tissue packet and extracted a new one. "A few things happened that shouldn't have happened. Touching and stuff. But I was never shared out, not like the others. Well, I was heavily pregnant by the time I got there, they wouldn't have wanted me."

Kate stared at her. "You were pregnant with Terry when you were at Marhaven?"

"No." Mary was shaking her head. "Not with Terry."

Kate was lost. "What do you mean – you mean you had another child before Terry?"

"He died." The words rang out with finality. Kate and Mary stared at each other across the table, steam rising from the teapot between them.

"You had another baby and he died?" Kate checked. Why had Mary never told her this before?

"He died when he was born," Mary said, almost to herself. She broke eye contact with Kate, looking away and off into the distance, clearly reliving her memories.

Kate shook her head, helplessly. "Mum, tell me about it from the beginning. You're saying you went to this children's home, this care home – why? Because you were pregnant?"

"Yeah. The social workers put me there, I didn't have anywhere else to go. I was only fifteen."

"It was one of those places where they used to put unmarried mothers?"

"Yeah, but not just that. They had other girls there too, runaways and orphans, people like that." Mary reached for her teacup and Kate tried not to notice her hand shaking or the stick thinness of her fingers. "Vulnerable girls. They knew nobody would believe them."

"So what are you saying happened, exactly? Sexual abuse?"

Mary flinched again. "I reckon. Something like that. Girls used to come in and every so often they'd be taken away in a big car. Someone told me that they used to get driven to a hotel and men would come to – you know..."

"Who told you?"

"Another girl at the home. Can't remember her name now, but she was there before I got there. She ran away though, one night. I guess she couldn't stand it anymore."

"You don't have any other evidence?" Kate could hear herself, sounding as though she was conducting a police interview, but she couldn't seem to stop herself. "Just the word of this other girl, this runaway?"

Mary dropped her eyes again. "I don't know – there was other stuff – it's hard to say what it was now though, but I remember feeling something was wrong, really wrong there."

She trailed off. Kate waited and then prompted her. "Like what?"

"I don't know," said Mary, looking close to tears. "There was something wrong there. But I was in a mess after the baby died, I didn't know whether I was coming or going. But there were other girls there who knew what was going on, they were all involved but no one believed them. We were helpless, no one wanted us. We tried to stick together, we wanted to be brave, but it's so hard when you've got no one on your side." Her voice sank and she muttered something else to herself, something that sounded like *Boudicca*.

For the first time, Kate found herself wondering about her mother's mental stability. Half of what Mary was muttering to herself seemed like a nightmare, a mish-mash of memory, fantasy and hallucination. She tried to get Mary to explain further but her mother shook her head, insisting that she couldn't remember any more. Eventually Kate gave up and poured her mother the last of the tea in the pot. Did it really matter, anyway? There was no evidence of a crime, nothing more to go on than a dying woman's memories which might be totally fabricated anyway. Kate winced at the brutality of her thoughts, but it was true, wasn't it? She had enough to worry about without wondering about a long-ago crime that may or may not have happened.

"I'll talk to Tin about it," she told her mother. "I'm sure he'll be able to explain better – I mean, I'm sure he'll be able to explain it all to me."

The conversation, such as it was, died after that. After the last drops of tea were drunk, both Kate and her mother began to make their excuses, talking over the top of one another.

"I've really got to get back—"

"Thanks for the tea, love but I've got to go—"

At the door to the tea room, Kate hesitated after helping her mother on with her coat. Then she made herself lean forward and kiss her mother's bony cheek. The flesh was cool beneath hers.

"I'll be in touch, Mum," she said. "Take care of yourself."

"You too," said Mary Redman. She turned and began to walk carefully down the steps to the pavement. "But then you always did that, didn't you? Always made sure you were okay, never mind anyone else."

She was gone before Kate could respond. Kate was only able to stand there on the top steps, with her mouth open like a fish, before anger and guilt began to mix in her stomach like a poisonous cocktail. Kate shut her mouth and began to walk back to where she'd parked her car, clenching her jaw all the way.

Chapter Twelve

THIS TIME, KATE PICKED THE restaurant for her dinner with Tin. As she walked through the door of The Boathouse, an Abbeyford pub that stood by the Avon River as it wound through the town park, she was assailed by doubt. It wasn't quite as nice as she remembered. How long had it been since she last came here? Kate thought back and realised it was probably over a year ago, when she and Olbeck had come here for a working lunch.

"Sorry," she said to Tin as she came up to him at the bar. "I remember this place being a lot nicer."

"It looks fine to me," said Tin, who was already perusing the menu. "They do steak and kidney pie. That's all I care about."

Kate grinned and ordered some drinks. They made their way over to the window seat, which did at least have a fine view of the Avon slipping past the terrace below. Kate watched the brown surface of the river twist and ripple with competing currents. A trio of mallard ducks floated by, almost in formation.

"The river's dropped a bit," Tin said, following her gaze. "Don't you think? We haven't had so much rain recently."

"Thank goodness." Kate looked up as the waitress approached with their starters. She was surprised at how easy it felt to be sat across from Tin, almost as if she were with a friend she'd known for years. All that marred the sense of comfortable familiarity were the butterflies that sparked in her stomach every time she caught his eye.

They chatted about the weather for a few moments longer. Kate mentioned that her best friend was getting married in a month's time and he was hoping for glorious sunshine. "Some hope," she said, spooning up some more risotto. "Still, if he and Jeff will insist on getting married in March, what do they expect?"

There was a flicker of surprise on Tin's face, quickly suppressed. "I've never been to a gay wedding before."

"No?" asked Kate, in a rather prickly tone. Surely he wasn't homophobic? She was mollified a second later when Tin added, "My gay friends aren't exactly the settling down type."

They concentrated on eating their meals for a few minutes. Kate was wondering where to begin in her questions. As it happened, Tin pre-empted her. "Mary said you two caught up the other day."

"Yes."

"She said you had some questions about Marhaven."

Kate wiped her mouth with her napkin and sat back. "That's putting it mildly."

"What has Mary told you?"

Kate recapped what her mother had said to her in the tea rooms the other night. She ended by asking, "She kept going on about these girls and being brave but nobody believed them. I couldn't make head nor tail of most of it, to be honest. What does she mean by that?"

Tin's normally cheerful face darkened. "Long story. I'll start at the beginning." He lined his cutlery up neatly in the middle of his plate and pushed it away from him. "Marhaven was built in the early nineteen twenties as a village school. It was a school up until the Second World War, when it remained empty for some years before being acquired by a church-funded charity group in the late nineteen sixties. They turned it into a care home for what were then termed 'unmarried mothers', although by the seventies, they were also taking in non-pregnant girls, a mixture of care-home cases, runaways and other children who needed to be cared for." He looked up at Kate. "Stop me if this begins to sound like a lecture."

"Stop," said Kate, unable to help herself. "No, I'm joking. Go on."

Tin did stop for a moment although he didn't smile. Instead he reached down to the rucksack he'd brought with him and brought out a thick manila folder. "These are some of my notes and research."

"Bloody hell," said Kate, taking it from him and weighing it in both hands. "You're quite thorough, aren't you?" She handed it back to him and said, joshingly, "Bit strange, though, bringing it all along on a date."

"Oh?" said Tin. "Is this what this is?"

There was a moment of silence as their eyes met across the table and Kate realised later that that was when the evening could have changed into something more...*interesting*. At the time, though, she was conscious merely of the usual pull-me-push-you sensations that she got when mixing business with pleasure. Half of her wanted to say 'sod the job' and merely please herself, move closer to Tin and throw caution to the wind. The other half, the half that never really gave up on the job, was shouting in her ear for her to stop mucking about and get on with what could be important professionally.

"What this exactly is, hasn't been ascertained yet," said Kate hastily but with a smile that was as flirtatious as she could make it. Tin returned it in kind. There was another charged moment and then Tin seemed to recollect himself, dipping his head towards the folder and placing it on the table in front of him. He's focused, thought Kate, recognising the same strength of purpose in Tin that she knew in herself. She didn't know whether that insight made her feel better or worse. He's ambitious, she told herself and something about that rang a faint warning bell. She sat back in her chair, business-like once more.

"Anyway," said Tin, clearly recollecting himself as well. "In the early nineteen seventies, two young girls, teenagers, made two separate accusations of sexual assault against the manager of Marhaven, Godfrey Peters. He and his sister, Melanie Peters, ran the care home together, under the auspices of the church charity."

"Okay," said Kate, feeling a little less giddy. "Do you have the reports there?"

"Somewhere. I'll dig them out in a second. Anyway, there were no charges brought in the end."

Kate rolled her eyes. "Okay."

Tin continued, "There was also a much more serious accusation levelled against the managers of the home by another girl a year or so after the first two reports. She accused Godfrey Peters of keeping her as a sex slave and essentially pimping her out to his friends."

Immediately Kate remembered her mother at the tea rooms the other night. *A few things happened that shouldn't have happened. Touching and stuff.*

But I was never shared out, not like the others... She repressed a shiver. "Go on," she said in a low tone, when Tin showed no signs of continuing.

Tin cleared his throat. "Pretty horrible accusations, as you can see. However, the problem here is that the accuser was clearly very mentally unwell. After she reported those claims to the police, she was immediately sectioned, or whatever the nineteen seventies equivalent was. She remained in the mental hospital for several years after that."

"What was her name?" asked Kate.

Tin consulted his notes. "That girl was Jane Moor. The other two girls who reported the alleged sexual assaults were called Tina Fetterton and Sarah Smith."

"And where are they all now? Have you talked to them?"

"I've tried to talk to Sarah Smith. She lives up north. She wouldn't say anything about Marhaven, or what might or might not have happened there. Just didn't want to know."

"And the others?"

"They're both dead. Jane Moor died of complications of pneumonia in nineteen ninety-five – she was an asthmatic – and Tina Fetterdon fell into Clifton Gorge in nineteen seventy-five."

Kate raised her eyebrows. "*Fell* into Clifton Gorge?"

"Well," said Tin. "Let's just say the coroner recorded an open verdict but everyone else seemed to think it was suicide. She was a very troubled young woman, apparently."

"Not surprising, really, is it?" said Kate. "If those accusations were true and nobody believed her?"

Tin sat forward again. "Exactly," he said with an urgency that surprised Kate. "That's what I'm talking about. That's what I'm investigating. What if those claims were true and yet no one did anything about it? What if Jane Moor's claims were true but no one believed her either, because they thought she was mad?"

"I know," said Kate slowly. "But where do you start? It's all so long ago."

"I know, and no one who was there is talking to me either." Tin rubbed both sides of his nose with his fingers, closing his eyes. He slumped back in his chair. "Oh, I don't know what I'm doing sometimes. Maybe it is pointless."

Kate felt a sharp surge of sympathy for him, knowing the feeling. "Don't give up yet," she said as encouragingly as possible.

"Yeah, I know," said Tin. "Anyway, if this really is a date, maybe I've talked enough about unpleasant things such as the Marhaven. Why don't I ask you a few more pertinent questions?"

"Such as what?" asked Kate, smiling.

"I'm going to get another drink and think of some really good ones," said Tin. "What can I get you?"

"Same again, thanks. Will you excuse me for a moment?"

Tin nodded as Kate got up. What was the etiquette for saying you needed the loo on a date? Kate wondered as she made for the stairs that led down to the toilets. Should she just have been bold and said 'I need a wee'? Or would that be a bit off-putting? It was so long since she'd been out with a man she couldn't remember what was done and not done on a first date.

Don't be ridiculous, she told herself, washing her hands. Her gaze was drawn to a poster stuck on the wall by the mirror, advertising a local club night. On the poster, the outline of a woman was drawn, raising her hands to the night sky beyond her. Kate stared at it. The outstretched tips of the woman's fingers reminded her of something. Should she ask? It would be such a long shot... She climbed the stairs, slowly, thinking.

"I've thought of one!" said Tin, waiting for her back at the table with two full glasses. "When—"

"Sorry," said Kate, interrupting him. "Can I just ask you something first? It's still about Marhaven, unfortunately."

"Sure."

Kate sat down. "Was there ever any record of a girl called Jean Tripp at the home?"

"Spelling?" asked Tin, reaching again for his folder. Kate obliged. Tin ruffled through various pages. "No – no, there wasn't."

"Oh well," said Kate. "It was a stupid idea anyw—"

"Wait, sorry – there was." Tin pointed to a line of text with his fore finger. "Sorry, she was known to the others there by another name, that's why I didn't pick her up immediately."

"*What*?" Kate was on her feet, transfixed. "Seriously? There was a girl at the Marhaven home called Jean Tripp?"

Tin looked up at her. "Yes. Yes, she's mentioned in statements several times. But she liked to be called Jonie, that's why I didn't immediately make the connection."

Jonie. The necklace. Kate sat back down abruptly, feeling as if all the strength had gone out of her legs.

"Why?" asked Tin.

Kate opened her mouth to tell him and shut it again abruptly. *He's a journalist, remember.* She thought he might actually make the connection, knowing the case that she was probably working on and given her obvious excitement. She forced herself to look cool and unruffled.

"Oh, it's just the name of someone who might be connected with a case I'm working on," Kate said casually. "Nothing serious. It was just a shot in the dark, really."

Beneath her calm exterior, she was fizzing with excitement. The fact that she was on a date with

Tin was momentarily forgotten. At that precise moment, all Kate wanted to do was call Olbeck. Could she get away with saying she had to make a phone call? She picked up her drink and took a long sip, thinking.

"What's going on?" asked Tin, his eyes narrowed. She might have known he'd be too intelligent to be fooled for long. Kate decided to come clean.

"Tin, I'm really sorry but there's a call I have to make. In fact, I've got a really early start so perhaps I should be making a move."

"Now?" Tin looked unconvinced. "Are you going to tell me why you're really going?"

Kate wavered. She really liked him, she didn't want to hurt him but... But sometimes work had to come first. "I can't explain right now. It's nothing to do with you – I mean, it's nothing that you've done. It's just – oh, I'll have to tell you later. I'll get this," she said, indicating the empty plates and glasses.

Tin snorted. "That's hardly the point. I thought we were going to start to get to know one another?"

"I know. I'm sorry. And we will. It's just – I do really have to go." Kate was immediately transported back to numerous scenes with Andrew Stanton: having to placate him for being out at work when he wanted her to be at home with him. Oh God, was this what all her relationships were going to be like? Do all men have this problem, she wondered. Probably not.

She forced herself to sit back down. After a moment, she reached over to take Tin's hand. The warmth of his fingers and the strength of his grip surprised her and once more she wavered. Did she really need to go tearing off to alert the team? Could she not just sit and enjoy the rest of the evening and not think about work for once? Kate considered it and rejected the idea. The fact was, excitement over Tin was one thing but excitement over a breakthrough in the case was another.

Tin still looked rather thunderous. Kate, on impulse, leant over the table and kissed him.

His mouth was stiff under hers for a moment and then relaxed. In a moment, they were kissing, really kissing, like schoolchildren who'd just discovered it for the first time. For a moment, the hubbub and swirl of the pub faded away and it was just the two of them, joined at the mouth and lost in one another.

Kate pulled back and they looked at one another. "I really do have to go," said Kate, somewhat breathlessly. "But I just – I just wanted..." She trailed off, her heart thumping.

Tin looked at her, with a tiny spark of amusement glimmering in his dark eyes. "Go on," he said eventually. "I'll take that as a positive sign."

"Do," said Kate. She kissed him again, more briefly this time but conscious of feeling it right down to her toes. "See you soon."

She grabbed up her bag and coat and turned,

making her way to the exit. It was cold outside, a chill night wind blowing, but she didn't feel it at all, wrapped in warmth all the way back to where she'd parked the car, walking along on feet that seemed to float, only barely touching the pavement.

Chapter Thirteen

"WHAT ARE YOU SMILING AT?"

Kate, caught out in a dream, re-running that kiss through her memory over and over again, started. "What's that?"

"You're grinning at nothing like a complete nutter," Theo said. He threw a plastic folder over the table at Kate who barely caught it in time. "What have you been up to?"

"What do you mean?"

Theo grinned. "I know that look. It's the one you get after a damn good seeing to." He smirked and then added, "All my ladies get it."

Kate became aware that she was perilously close to blushing. "Oh, sod off, Theo. When are you actually going to grow up and have a proper relationship, not just a load of friends with benefits?"

She became aware that she sounded a lot more defensive that she had planned to. Theo grinned even more. Kate added, "How many 'lay-dees' are you up to now, anyway?"

Theo looked smug. "About four on the go."

Kate rolled her eyes. "I don't know where you find the energy."

"Four what?" Fliss asked cheerfully, as she walked up to the desks with a pile of paperwork in her hands.

"Don't ask," said Kate. "Theo's just showing off, as usual." She picked up the plastic folder he'd just thrown at her and looked at it. "Have you actually been doing some work for once? What are these?"

"Read 'em," Theo said, picking up his empty mug and getting up. "Statements from Jackie Tripp for starters. Rav and I have been busy up in Sheffield while you've been getting lucky." Kate threw a paperclip at him and he ducked and grinned, sauntering off towards the coffee machine.

"Cheeky bastard," muttered Kate, bending her head towards the statements. Something to read through now while she waited for Olbeck. She looked up to check his office once more, but it remained stubbornly empty. Where was he? Had he told Anderton yet?

"You might also want a look at these," said Fliss, holding out another bunch of folders.

"What are they?"

"Medical records for Jean Tripp. They were couriered down this morning."

"Thanks, Fliss." Kate thought of the thousands – millions – of words she'd have to wade through today and suppressed a groan. "Better get started, I suppose."

Fliss offered to make her a coffee and Kate accepted gratefully. She was beginning to warm to the newest member of the team. For one thing, Fliss at least was not about to boast of her many sexual conquests, or Kate didn't think so. Dismissing the irrelevant musings, Kate forced herself to concentrate on the mountain of paperwork before her.

She began with the medical records. Jean Tripp had been born in nineteen fifty-eight, the third daughter of parents who were approaching middle age when she was born. The usual childhood illnesses were documented, as was the fractured arm that Jackie Tripp had mentioned and that the post mortem had found. There was nothing much untoward in the records until Jean reached the age of twelve. Then a note of discord could be ascertained, creeping into the official jargon of the doctor's notes: bruising from a fight in the school playground, several urinary infections, a prescription for sleeping tablets. Kate read on, frowning a little. After a while, she looked through the paperwork that Rav and Theo had managed to track down from Jean's old secondary school. As she read through it, a definite picture emerged; of a troubled girl, who could be violent, a girl who up until the age of twelve seemed to have had a normal, happy, untroubled childhood. So what had happened? The onset of puberty? Getting in with a bad crowd? Drug use or alcohol abuse? Kate riffled through the remaining pages. The signs were there but what did they point to, and who could they ask now? She got up, stretched and sat back down again, reaching for Jackie Tripp's statement.

Jean was my older sister by four years. Our parents were Doreen and Stanley Tripp, who were married in 1949. Our father worked in Benson's, the local paint factory, up until his death from lung cancer in 1965 and our mother married again two years later. Jean didn't get on with our new stepfather, John Billson, and they would have frequent arguments. Jean would sometimes run away but would always be brought home again by the police. In 1971, when she was fourteen, she left home without telling our parents but she told me before she left she was going to London to try and become a model. She had always had an interest in acting and singing. After that time, I did not see her again but some years later, possibly in 1973 or 1974, a postcard arrived from her, typed but with her signature at the bottom, telling us that she was moving to Spain and would try and visit us before she went. Jean never did visit us and there was no more communication between us.

Was that it? Kate turned the page over to see if there was anything on the back and was met by blank space. She sighed and looked up at Theo. "Is this really all that Jackie Tripp could tell you?"

Theo looked up from his report. "Listen, it was

an effort even to get her to say that much. She's not exactly the sharpest knife in the drawer, is she?"

"No," Kate admitted. She looked again at the few paragraphs of type. The mention of the stepfather was interesting. Kate worked out the dates in her head. If Doreen Tripp had remarried when Jean was eight, that would explain the gradual decline in her behaviour, if Jean and her stepfather had been at loggerheads. But was that all it was? Kate read through the medical notes again, her eye snagging on the record of several urinary infections. She bit her lip. That could suggest something much worse...

She caught a flicker of movement out of the corner of her eye and looked up. Olbeck was back and he and Anderton were both beckoning her from the office doorway. Kate shot out of her seat.

"My office," Anderton said and wheeled around. Kate and Olbeck hurried after him.

"So," said Anderton, when they were all seated in his office – or rather, Kate and Olbeck were seated and watching their boss pace up and down. "How the hell did you manage to track that little piece of info down, Kate?"

"A journalistic contact," said Kate, loftily. She thought that might sound a bit more professional than saying 'from a bloke I really do quite want to sleep with'.

Anderton raised his eyebrows. "And this contact is legit?"

"I think so. Obviously we're going to have to corroborate the evidence."

Anderton continued his pacing. "Well, I can't imagine that would take much time. Perhaps we need to start looking a bit more closely at this so-called care home. It's not still in use as that sort of facility, is it?"

"I don't think so," Kate said, wishing she'd asked Tin that very question.

"Okay. Well, that will do for starters. Find out everything you can about it. Talk to your journalistic contact." Kate met Anderton's eye and fought not to blush. "Presumably they'll have plenty of information on it. See if you can pull any records relating to Jean Tripp and any known contacts. Try and talk to someone who might have known her, if there is anyone. Find the people who ran the facility, if they're still alive, and question them." He finally came to a halt and threw himself into his desk chair, churning his thick grey hair with one hand. "That's all I can think of for now but if anyone else has anything to add...?"

"I'll talk to Kate back in my office," said Olbeck, getting up. "I know you've got stuff to do."

"Never busier. Okay, I'll talk to you both later."

Kate and Olbeck were almost at his office door before Anderton added "I'm sure you're aware of this, but keen as I am to get this case closed, be aware that I don't have an unlimited budget."

Kate turned to stare at him. He shrugged, looking a little uncomfortable and said "I just had to point that out. You of all people, both of you, know how stretched we are."

Olbeck and Kate exchanged a look. "We understand," Olbeck said a moment later.

"Good," Anderton said, dismissing them with a wave of his hand. "Off you go."

"What was *that* all about?" Kate said, once they were back in Olbeck's office with the door shut.

"God knows."

"We're always on a limited budget," Kate said. She wandered around the office, looking out onto the busy floor through the glass walls. "Why did he feel he had to point that out?"

"Kate, I don't know." Olbeck seated himself at his desk and clicked the mouse to bring the computer screen to life. "Maybe we're on more than a usually restricted budget."

"Maybe," Kate said. She frowned and said, "It was almost..."

"What?" prompted Olbeck, as she trailed off.

"I don't know. Almost like he was warning us off."

Olbeck gave Kate a puzzled look. "I think you might be reading a little bit too much into it."

"Maybe," Kate said, once more. Then she shrugged and said "I'm going to make a start, anyway."

"Nice one." Olbeck rolled his chair nearer to his computer. Kate gave him a casual salute in farewell and was almost out the door before Olbeck said "Oh, by the way, have you done your speech yet? It's just that Jeff keeps nagging me—"

"Almost finished it!" Kate lied smartly. "I'll run through it with you tomorrow. No, maybe the day after tomorrow."

Hastening back to her desk, she groaned inwardly. That bloody speech: She'd have to make a start on that tonight, exhaustion or no exhaustion. Feeling tired at the very thought, she sat back down again at her desk and bent her head towards the many folders, determined to make a dent in the paperwork.

Later that evening, Kate put down her empty dinner plate on the living room coffee table, pushed Merlin away as he went to investigate the leftovers and pulled a notepad and pen towards her. She wrote 'speech' in large letters at the top of the page, underlined the word several times with vigour, sat up straighter with pen poised in her fingers – and then collapsed against the back of the sofa, groaning aloud.

Think, Kate, think. *I first met Mark when...* no, too clichéd. *I knew Mark and Jeff would be a happy couple when...* when what? Grimacing, she scrolled through her memories, trying to find the one definitive recollection that would kick-start her speech, leaving people hanging on to her every word and not doing what most people normally do during the wedding speeches, which is surreptitiously drink more and pray for them all to be over.

After fifteen minutes, the sum total of which yield three stilted sentences, Kate flung her pen down, swearing. Then she picked it up and wrote 'DO IT TOMORROW!' in flaring capital letters, picked Merlin up and went up the stairs to bed.

Chapter Fourteen

THE PILE OF PAPERWORK FOR the Jean Tripp case
seemed to have tripled overnight. Kate, Theo, Jane
and Fliss shared it out between them and sat back
down at their desks, with the grim demeanour of
those who knew a decent lunch break would be a
distant dream.

Kate opened the first report, which turned out
to be the victim statements from the two girls who
had reported Godfrey Peters for sexual assault
back in the seventies. The foremost one was the
report from Tina Fetterdon. Kate read through it
carefully, noting the accusations: touching her
breasts, touching her genitals, forced fellatio. Kate
grimaced, looked at Tina Fetterdon's date of birth
and worked out Tina would have been fourteen
at the time she accused Godfrey Peters. Briefly,
Kate recalled an earlier case she'd worked, another
abuse case culminating in the deaths of two people.
From there, her mind skipped back to Jean Tripp's
medical reports. What if Jean Tripp's stepfather had

been abusing her? Was that why she ran away from home?

Kate read on, working her way through the report from Sarah Smith. Much the same as Tina Fetterdon's accusations. Why the hell hadn't it been properly followed up? Two girls reporting the same person for the same crimes – surely that warranted a decent investigation at least? It was the seventies, Kate reminded herself, thinking about all the hideous things several famous men had done at the time to hundreds – if not thousands – of children. People got away with things.

She looked at the name of the officer who'd filed each report. The first, a Kevin Doherty, drew a blank, but the second made her frown. Norman Chambers. Now why was that familiar? Kate sat, thinking for a moment before she realised. Why of course, Norman Chambers, a detective sergeant at the time of the report, had ended up being Detective Superintendent Chambers. She'd even met him once, when he visited her in hospital when she'd been recuperating from the attack that nearly killed her, three years ago. He'd retired soon after that, but he was still seen at the yearly Abbeyford Police fundraiser and occasionally in the office. Kate could recall him now, a rather lantern-faced man, with tufty white eyebrows and equally white hair arranged in a patrician crest.

She shook herself mentally and brought herself back to the present. Would it be worth trying to get an interview with Norman Chambers, to see if he could remember anything about the interviews with these girls? Kate knew Anderton and he were friendly; Chambers had once been Anderton's direct superior, if she remembered correctly. Kate made a note to ask Anderton whether he thought it was a good idea.

Okay. One thing to do. Kate scribbled notes as other ideas occurred to her. The first was one that she almost discounted out of hand, purely because of her emotional reaction to it. Then she told herself not to be so ridiculous. She would contact her mother and see if Mary could recall anything, anything at all about Jean Tripp – Jonie.

Kate put her pen down for a second, realising she'd not moved from her desk in over an hour. She stretched, groaning, catching Theo's eye.

"Anything, mate?" he asked.

Kate always found it rather endearing when he called her mate. "A few leads." She explained about Norman Chambers, ending with the question, "Think he'd talk to us about what happened?"

Theo's dark eyebrows rose rapidly. "Hmm... well, worth a try, maybe." He was silent for a second and then added "We might be just a little bit too low down on the scale, though."

Kate frowned. "I'm not going to *interrogate* him, just ask him if he remembers anything."

"It's over forty years ago. I'd hazard a guess he'll remember the sum total of fuck all."

Kate blew out her cheeks. "Yes, well. You're probably right." She stood up, stretched again and asked "So, what about you? Anything?"

"I think we should be interviewing Melanie Peters. If she's still alive and *compos mentis*."

Kate immediately thought of Tin and how he'd tried to do exactly that. Mind you, she and Theo had the might of the law on their side. "Yes, that's probably a good idea."

They both returned to their desks and bent over the folders again. At lunch time, Fliss offered to go and do a McDonalds run, for which Kate, much as she deplored fast food, could have kissed her. She remembered being the newly qualified rookie in Bournemouth; all those endless rounds of tea-making and sandwich buying, hoping to find her place in the team, hoping to be accepted. A secondary thought was that, to date, she hadn't really made much effort to be friendly to Fliss, to be inclusive and welcoming. *Bad Kate*. She made a resolution that that would change.

Buoyed by her good intentions, Kate called her mother. The phone went to voicemail again so Kate left what she hoped was a friendly, casual sort of message, that nevertheless implied that Kate would really like to talk to Mary again soon. Of course, she didn't mention Marhaven or anything like that. Putting her mobile down, she tapped a pen against the side of her jaw, thinking. What next?

Her thoughts were interrupted by the crash of the office door being flung back on its hinges as Anderton strode into the room. Olbeck came to the door of his office, obviously in enquiry. Kate and the rest of the team turned their chairs to face their boss.

"Nothing to panic about, people," said Anderton. "But the identification of Jean Tripp goes public today. It'll be in the national and the regional press, so be prepared for a deluge of calls from people claiming they knew her, that they know who killed her, how she was abducted by aliens who then buried her – you know the drill."

Kate smiled reluctantly. Anderton raised a hand and said, "That's all, folks. We'll catch up later," and began to walk back to the corridor. Kate jumped up and followed him out.

"Hello," he said, as she caught up with him. "What's up?"

With Anderton, Kate was never quite sure whether he meant that question as a personal or a professional enquiry. Consequently, she never quite knew how to answer him. She mumbled something as they went into his office and both sat down. Kate, looking at him across the table, wondered whether he was still seeing the beautiful blonde who'd visited the office all those months ago. How that had hurt at the time. She was pleased to realise that now the thought didn't give her more than a moment of uneasiness. Relaxing a little, she smiled at him across the desk.

"I've got a quick question," she said.

"Yes?"

Kate explained about the reports and the fact that Norman Chambers had been the officer on the record at the time of the accusations. "So, I was wondering if you think it would be a good idea to talk to him?" she finished, leaning forward a little in her chair.

Anderton was still for a moment, obviously thinking. Kate, practiced at reading his face, could have sworn that, just for a second, there was something like a flash of uneasiness. Just a second's worth of anxiety. It was gone in an instant, fast enough for her to have doubted that she'd seen it.

"Yes, sounds like something worth doing," Anderton said, after a moment.

"Great," Kate said. "Could you give me his address?"

"There's just one thing," said Anderton. "It might be easier if I do it. I mean, no offence, Kate, but this is a highly decorated former officer we're talking about. And he's a friend of mine."

Kate frowned. "I only want to talk to him, briefly really – see if he remembers anything."

"I know, I know. But you know how it is – hierarchy and so forth. He'll probably be a lot more receptive to having a chat with me."

Kate swallowed. What Anderton was saying made sense, of course it did, but... There was something underneath it all, just a finger of uneasiness that nudged her. It was too nebulous a feeling for Kate to truly be able to identify just what it was that made her uneasy.

She brushed it aside. "That's fine," she said breezily. "I understand. No problem."

"It'll be a good chance to catch up with the old bugger, actually," Anderton said, sitting back in his chair. "Haven't seen him for months. Leave it with me and I'll see if I can see him sometime this week. How are things going, anyway? Anything else to report?"

Kate sat forward again, taking Anderton through her list of things to do. He listened with his usual attention and Kate spoke quite normally but, underneath it all, she was still aware of that faint hint of uneasiness, like a cold draught, a tiny stream of cool air from a source that was undetectable.

Back at her desk, she tried to shake the feeling off. She had two missed calls on her mobile, one from her mother and one from Tin. Kate hesitated and listened to the voicemail from her mother first. Mary Redman, voice huskier and weaker than ever, left a hesitant message saying that she would be in hospital for treatment for the next couple of days but would like to talk to Kate again anyway. Kate frowned. Which hospital was it? Surely she should go and visit her mother, if she had any compassion, after all. I must call Jay, she thought, and the others, and see what they think. Then she brought up the missed call from Tin and dialled into the voicemail he'd left her.

"Kate, it's me." Had they reached such terms of intimacy already? Kate was both pleased and alarmed by the thought. She listened further. "Could we meet up again? Not just because you owe me a decent dinner." Kate smiled reluctantly at that. "I've got some info that might prove...fruitful. Hell, I just want to talk it over with someone, really. No, that's not true. I want to talk it over with you. Let me know where and when, okay? If they do a decent steak and kidney pie, that's a bonus."

Kate smiled again and pressed the button to end the call. There was something to be said for mixing business with pleasure, she mused, already wondering where she could suggest for dinner. She tried to ignore the tiny voice that piped up that she didn't really know the man from Adam, and the fact that he was an investigative journalist meant that she really ought to be going into this with her eyes wide open. *Oh, sod it.* Kate dialled Tin's number, got his voicemail and left him a message telling him that she'd be free for a sumptuous dinner that evening at The Black Cat, if he was free. She put the phone down, fighting down a smile that wanted to become a beam.

TIN WAS WAITING FOR HER as before, thankfully this time unaccompanied by Kate's mother. He caught sight of her as she came through the doorway and waved. Kate walked up to him rather self-consciously. Was she supposed to kiss him? There was an awkward moment of hesitancy and then Tin leant forward and pecked her cheek. "Hello."

"Hello." Kate threw her hair back in apparent unconcern and sat down. She was remembering the kiss they'd shared at their previous meeting. Had Tin thought that that had been a mistake? Was he cooling off? Get a grip, she told herself – not for the first time.

"You look good," Tin added.

Kate struggled not to show how pleased that remark made her. "Thanks," she said, coolly, and added, "so do you." Their eyes met once more, and Kate felt very surely then that Tin was in no danger of cooling off.

She forced herself to drag her gaze away. "What was it you wanted to talk about?"

Tin seemed to recollect himself too. "I see you've released the name of the victim in the Munford Gorge case." He held her gaze for a beat and then added, "What a coincidence."

Kate was too old a hand at this to blush. "Well, I have to thank you for an excellent lead. It really brought things forward."

Tin half-laughed. "I'm starting to think you're just meeting up with me for my journalistic skills."

"That too," said Kate and winked at him.

"Seriously, though, I couldn't mention it to you then. I can't talk about the case now, so if that's why you wanted to meet me, then I'm afraid we're going to have to call it a night right now."

"All right, all right," said Tin, sounding a little offended. "God, I never knew you coppers were such hard work."

"Now who's getting defensive?" said Kate, conscious of a spurt of annoyance. They both realised they'd gone from doe-eyed looks to glares across the table and both looked away. Kate felt suddenly quite depressed. Why was she never seemingly able to make a relationship work? Not that this one had even so much as got off the ground... She stared down at the table for a moment before realising that Tin was asking her if she wanted a drink. "Okay, then," she said and then pulled herself up with a jerk, realising how sullen and grudging she sounded. She looked up at him again.

"Look," she said. "This hasn't gone according to plan, and it's probably my fault. I'm sorry." There you go, Magda, she thought. All that hard work was finally paying off. *I'm finally able to admit when I'm wrong.* "Perhaps we shouldn't talk about Marhaven, or anything else to do with the case. Perhaps we should just talk about – oh, I don't know – about normal things. The sort of things everyone else talks about when they meet up for a drink."

Tin had listened to her speech with an impassive

face which gradually softened into something approaching his normal, cheerful demeanour. Once she'd finished speaking, he said "Well, you're probably right. Let's have a drink and be normal for once."

"Right!" said Kate, sitting back in her chair. She watched Tin go to the bar and order the drinks, forcing herself to relax back into her seat, trying to get herself into a 'normal' frame of mind. The trouble was, as she became acutely aware, that she realised she really did want to know what it was he had to tell her about the case.

Tin sat back down again with their drinks and Kate, unable to help herself, said "Look, I know we just agreed not to talk about it but what was it that you wanted to tell me?"

Tin burst out laughing. "You're unbelievable, you are. I thought I was wedded to my career, but you're even worse."

Kate laughed despite herself. "Well, at least you're getting to know this up front. No hidden surprises further down the line."

Tin gave her an amused glance. "Well, as it happens, I also want to talk about it, but being too much of a gentleman, I had to wait until you gave me the option." They both exchanged smiles that acknowledged their mutual weakness. "Now," said Tin, becoming business-like. "Like I said, you've named the victim of the Munford Gorge case as Jean Tripp, right?"

"Right."

"Well, a day after that became public knowledge, I had a call from a guy who used to be a journalist for the Abbeyford Gazette, years ago. He's retired now, but he used to cover quite a lot of reporting for them and for some of the other regional newspapers."

"Okay," said Kate, taking a sip of her drink.

Tin continued, "This guy – his name's Tom, Tom Marks – he told me that he'd been contacted by Jean Tripp in the early seventies because she wanted to give him an exclusive on some big scandal involving the Marhaven home. Apparently she didn't want to go into details over the phone but she sounded legit enough, so he arranged to meet her in a few days' time in person."

Tin stopped talking for a moment to gulp his drink. "And?" prompted Kate after a moment.

"Well, that's just it. Apparently Jean Tripp never turned up. Tom Marks knew that she was living at the Marhaven care home, and after a few days he made some discreet enquiries and was told that Jean had run away. That was apparently that."

"And?" said Kate, sensing there was more.

"You'll have to meet this guy, Tom, and you'll see what he means. Apparently, he didn't like it, this supposed run-away. Something about it just didn't quite sit right, he said. So he started doing a bit more digging, trying to talk to a couple of the other girls there, that sort of thing."

"Why hasn't he come to us?" demanded Kate.

Tin looked uncomfortable. "Well, he had his reasons. Like I said, it's probably best if you contact him yourself. He may or may not tell you what he told me."

Kate sat back and stared at Tin. "Are you being deliberately obtuse? Why the big mystery?"

Tin dropped his gaze to the beermat he was turning around and around in his hands. "There's no mystery," he said after a moment. "It's probably best if you talk to him yourself, that's all."

Kate set her teeth in annoyance. Then she sat forward and said abruptly, "All right."

"Okay," said Tin "So if I—"

"Let's go," said Kate. "We'll go and see him now."

Tin's eyes bulged. "What? Now?" He risked a look at his watch. "It's almost ten."

"So call him and tell him we're on our way. I assume he lives locally?"

"Yes, but—" Tin looked up at Kate as she stood up and began gathering up her things. "Seriously? You want to talk to him now?"

"Yes, I do. And seeing as you're the one who brought him to my attention, it's probably best you come along too."

"Blimey, I..." Tin trailed off and then seemed to collect himself, getting up and pulling on his coat. "You don't mess about, do you?"

"Not in things like this." Kate stood back to let him move past her. "I'll drive if you'll show me the way."

Chapter Fifteen

Tom Marks lived in a small terraced house on the outskirts of Abbeyford. He seemed unsurprised to have two relative strangers arriving on his doorstep at ten fifteen in the evening, but Tin had managed to talk to him as they drove towards his house and give him a little bit of warning. Kate had said nothing as she listened to their conversation, but she'd heard enough to hear a faint nervousness in the disembodied voice of Tom Marks as it was heard issuing from Tin's mobile.

Tom Marks was a small man, thin but wiry, with a pair of black-framed, John Lennon glasses. He was totally bald and wore a grey cashmere sweater and a pair of dark denim jeans. He obviously lived alone, in a house stuffed full of books, papers, pictures and plants that was nonetheless homely and comfortable.

He shook Kate's hand and glanced at her warrant card, which she presented as a matter of course. She was aware of Tin's swift glance at it too. "Pleased to meet you," Tom Marks said, adding, "that's not something I thought I'd ever find myself saying to a police officer, to be honest."

Kate said nothing but noted the remark. They moved into a small front room, with a fire flickering cosily in the brick grate. Tom seated himself in a brown leather chair, clearly the one he used every day, and left Tin and Kate to find themselves a seat on the small sofa. Kate glanced at Tin, hoping to indicate that she would lead the talking and after a moment, he raised his eyebrows and sat back in acquiescence.

"I understand that you were contacted by someone you believed to be Jean Tripp, Mr Marks? When exactly was this?"

Tom Marks didn't reply for a moment. He leant forward, poked the fire and then said, with his face turned away, "Is this off the record?"

"You're not under caution, Mr Marks."

He nodded, apparently satisfied. "It's probably best if I tell you what happened from start to finish. Then you can question me further if you think it necessary."

"As you wish," said Kate, shifting a little on the sofa to face him more fully.

Tom Marks added another log to the fire and then sat back himself, crossing one neat leg over the other. "It's been so long since it happened, it's almost a lifetime ago. But it's funny, as soon as I heard her name I was transported straight back there, almost as if the intervening years had never happened. I suppose it was because it was the first time in my life I'd been truly frightened. The first time in my adult life, I mean." He was silent for a moment and then continued. "I was working for the Abbeyford Gazette at the time. It was nineteen seventy three, I remember that distinctly. As soon as I heard you were coming over, I looked up my notebooks from that time. I always kept them – like I said, it made a great impression on me."

"Why did you not come straight to us, Mr Marks?" said Kate, unable to help the question.

He glanced at her and frowned. "That will be made perfectly obvious as I go along. Please, let me continue."

"Sorry," said Kate. "Please go on."

He inclined his head in acknowledgement of her apology. "Like I said, I was working at the Abbeyford Gazette at the time. I was their crime correspondent, for what that was worth – we hardly had a lot of serious crime then, or so you would think." He thought for a moment and then went on. "I'm sure there was just as much evil and depravity in the world then as there is now, but it was far more hidden. People got away with things then."

Kate's thoughts exactly. She leaned forward a little, intent on Tom Mark's words.

He went on. "Jean Tripp rang me one day, in

June, I think it was. She was quite distressed, quite upset but very – how can I put it – very earnest in what she was saying. Very sincere. She told me that she had certain knowledge of a very serious crime taking place at the Marhaven care home and that she wanted to talk to me about it, to 'get it all out in the open before it was too late'. Those were her exact words, I remember them as if it were yesterday."

Tom Marks again fell silent. Kate wondered whether she dared interrupt him but this time, Tin did it for her.

"What exactly were her accusations?" Tin asked.

Tom Marks didn't answer for a moment. Then he said with sadness in his voice "She told me that the girls in Marhaven care home were used as sex slaves and pimped out to different men in a kind of paedophile ring. She didn't use that term, I'm not sure it was even in common knowledge at that time, but looking back, that's what she meant. She said that the men that used the girls were from some of the most respectable places in Abbeyford, teachers, lawyers, etcetera. Godfrey Peters, who ran the home, would arrange for the girls to be delivered to special parties at secret locations. Jean told me that she was one of these girls and that she'd been raped and abused at these parties by men who were otherwise pillars of the community. I'm paraphrasing, of course, but that's what it came down to."

Nobody said anything. After a moment, Tom

Marks began to speak once more. "I believed her. Or, let me be clearer, I was sufficiently concerned as to want to talk to Jean further. So we arranged to meet in a few days' time. I asked her to meet me in a coffee bar in Abbeyford, but she didn't want to, she said she was scared of being followed, so we arranged to meet somewhere in Bristol, a pub near the docks."

Unable to help herself, Kate interrupted. "She said she was scared of being followed?"

Tom Marks nodded. "She was quite scared, quite paranoid. There may have been a good reason for that, as I found out later, but it could have been because she truly was afraid that someone was following her. Anyway, we arranged the meeting, and on the day I went to the venue we'd decided on and waited. And waited and waited. She never turned up." He turned to poke the fire once more and they all watched the orange sparks flower up into the darkness of the chimney. "I didn't have a contact number for her but I knew she was living at the Marhaven home. I waited to see if she would contact me again, but a week went by and there was nothing." He paused once more and said "To be honest, at first I thought she'd got cold feet. That Jean had been lying about what she'd told me and she'd got scared of the repercussions."

There was a short silence. Kate cleared her throat and asked "But something must have made you start looking for her? Tin—" She gave him a glance and he returned it, half-smiling. "Tin said that you made some enquiries at the home?"

Tom Marks nodded. He'd been sitting hunched forward in his chair, as if cold and needing the warmth of the fire. Now he sat back, easing his shoulders as if they were stiff and painful. "After a few weeks, I started to get a bit worried. It was her distress, you see, when she called me. She sounded – I don't know, desperate. And if what she had told me was true, then it was possible that she was in some danger. So I thought about it and after a while I decided to see if I could find her."

"How did you do that?" asked Kate.

Tom gave a grunt of a laugh. "I posed as a documentary film maker. I went to see Godfrey Peters and his sister and told them I was making a Christian documentary on the wayward youth of today."

"They believed you?" asked Tin.

"Apparently. They certainly weren't worried about telling me that they had several 'problem girls' at the home and one of them had recently run away."

"Jean," Kate said; a statement rather than a question.

Tom nodded. "They told me it wasn't the first time. Apparently she was a runaway from her family home and had ended up at Marhaven having been on the streets. They told me she had drug and alcohol problems, which they were trying to arrange for her to have treatment for. I asked if they'd reported the fact that she was missing to the police and they told me they had."

Kate, listening intently, frowned. If what Tom was saying were true, then the Peters had been lying, about that if nothing else.

Tom was still speaking. "I talked to some of the other girls there, or I tried to. I left my contact number for several of them and told them that Jean had talked to me and to get in touch with me if they had anything to tell me. I told the Peters that it was because I might need to interview them for the documentary."

"Did any of them get in touch?" asked Kate.

Tom shook his head. "No. No, they didn't." He looked again into the depths of the fire once more and then turned back to face them. "Would anyone like a drink?"

Kate and Tin both declined but Tom went on to say "Well, I'll go ahead and have one, if you don't object. I could do with one, for this part of the story."

Kate and Tin both murmured something along the lines of that being no problem. Tom left the room for a moment and came back after a few minutes, carrying what looked like a glass of whisky. He sat back down again, sighing.

"Hardly drink spirits these days," he said. "Not like in my reporting days. My God, we used to throw it back then. Amazing I'm still here, really." He took a sip, grimacing, and then a longer one, swallowing the liquid down as if it were medicine. Then he put the glass down and leant forward. "It was about a week after I'd been to Marhaven and talked to the girls. I was coming back from town, quite late – I think I'd been reporting on a traffic accident or something like that. I was just outside of Abbeyford – I lived in Cudston Magna then, right out in the middle of nowhere. So I'm driving down these dark country lanes and suddenly there's a flashing blue light in my rear view mirror."

The fire had died down once more. The room seemed to gather shadows, the warm light from the fire dimming so that Kate found it suddenly hard not to shiver.

Tom went on, glass in one hand. "Once I'd pulled over and wound my window down, this officer appeared. I didn't recognise him but he was a big chap, broad-shouldered. I didn't think to look at his badge number or anything like that, you just didn't think about those things in those days. It was dark, anyway, pitch black with no streetlights. He said something like 'Going a bit fast for these roads, weren't you, sir?'" Tom stretched his shoulders back again and went on. "Of course, I hadn't been. I knew how dangerous those roads could be, especially at night. I said something to that effect and that's when it stopped being a nuisance and started being something that I thought could – could escalate. He ordered me to get out of the car and stand with my hands on the bonnet and then he started searching the car, all the while telling me to shut up, because, of course, I was protesting at this point, because as far as I could see I'd done nothing wrong." Tom lifted up the glass to his lips and drained it. Coughing, he went on. "It seemed to go on for ever. It was cold, I remember that, for a summer night. I remember feeling my fingers go numb on the metal of the car. Eventually, the officer came up to me and held something in my face, a small plastic bag full of white powder and he said, something like, 'What's all this, then?'"

Kate leant forward herself, watching Tom closely. "What was it?"

Tom shrugged. "I presume it was cocaine, or something like that. Whatever it was, it certainly didn't belong to me. The closest I ever got to narcotics was marijuana. Anyway, the upshot of it was this officer was going to charge me for possession. For something that wasn't even mine."

There was another moment of silence.

"Are you saying you think he planted it on you – in your car?" asked Kate, just to be sure.

Tom seemed to shake himself a little, as if waking himself from a dream. "Well, it's the only explanation that fits, isn't it? It wasn't mine and none of my friends would have dreamt of leaving something so incriminating in plain view. But what really made me realise what had happened was that the policeman used it as a threat. He was ranting about court and prison and things like that – I remember the clouds of steam puffing into the air as he yelled at me - but then he calmed down and told me that he could find a way to let me off – if I learnt how to behave myself. And that meant keeping my nose out of things that didn't concern me."

Tin leant forward. Kate saw the pink tip of his tongue moisten his lips and wondered if his mouth was as dry as hers. "Did he mention Marhaven specifically?" Tin asked.

Tom shook his head. "No. No, nothing that specific. To be honest, at that point, I was so shaken I wasn't really thinking about anything like that. I just wanted to get home without being arrested." He sat back in his seat with a sigh. "Anyway, eventually he let me go, once I'd grovelled enough. I drove home very slowly. I was shaking." He looked down at his hands, clutching one another. "The next day I thought it over and I wondered what was going on. Had I just run up against one bad apple, or was I poking about in things that were too dangerous to go on investigating?"

The three of them were silent once more, looking at the sunset glow of the fire.

"So did you drop it? Like he told you too?" Kate asked eventually.

Tom looked grim. "I tried contacting some of the girls at Marhaven once more, just once. Then I woke up one morning to find all my tires slashed. I got the message after that. I left it all well alone." He shifted in his seat. "I kept trying to tell myself that it could have been due to something else – I was reporting on several cases that year, at least one of which was gang-related – but – I don't know – it just left a nasty taste in my mouth. It haunted me, you might say. That's why, when I heard that the body you'd found was Jean Tripp, I knew I had to tell *somebody*. But you can see why I didn't – I don't – want to go to the police."

"You can't surely think..." Kate trailed off. She was thinking back herself, back to that faint sense of uneasiness that she'd recently felt pervading the case as she worked. What was wrong? Was it... There was nothing she could put her finger on, nothing concrete; it was all too faint, a cobweb of doubt.

"Did you ever find out who that officer was?" asked Tin.

Tom nodded. "Naturally. That was almost the first thing I did. His name was Kevin Doherty." Kate gave a small start of surprise and she saw that both Tin and Tom had noticed. Neither asked her to explain though. Tom went on. "Let's just say I followed his career from then on, with interest, you could say. He was not a pleasant man."

"What happened to him?" asked Kate, knowing she'd have to look into this herself.

"He was dismissed from the force in nineteen eighty because of an accusation of sexual misconduct with a suspect. No charges were actually brought." Tom paused and then added, "He died in a hit and run accident that same year. They never found the culprit."

Kate wondered whether she could ask him to elaborate but decided against it. It would be something to investigate at work tomorrow. The thought of work made her realise quite how late it was, past midnight. They'd been sat here for hours. She glanced at Tin, hoping to make him understand, indicating with a nod of her head her wristwatch. He nodded.

"Mr Marks, you've been so helpful," said Kate, "but it's getting late and I think we're going to have to call it a night. There's just one thing." She hesitated, unsure of the reception her question would receive. "Would you be willing to make a statement to the effect of everything you've just told me – us?"

Tom looked at her without speaking for a moment. She could see his eyes behind the glass of his spectacles, dark and watchful. "Well, I suppose that depends, doesn't it?"

"Depends?" asked Kate

He looked directly at her. "Depends on who's in charge."

They said goodnight soon after that, and Tin and

Kate walked back to the car. Both were silent. Kate turned the heater of the car up to full as she pulled away from the kerb, hunching herself back into her seat. She felt colder than the night's temperature warranted. "Where am I dropping you?" she asked Tin, the first words either of them had spoken for ten minutes.

She could see Tin looking at her and she wondered whether he'd expected to be invited back to her place for the night. Well, if he had, he'd be disappointed. She was far too tired and emotionally wrung out from the night's conversation to even think of anything amorous.

"You can just drop me back at my car," said Tin, quite coolly, as if she were a vague acquaintance.

Kate was conscious of a feeling of sadness, of another wasted opportunity, but she was just too limp with fatigue to do anything about it. She thanked him for his help colourlessly, and he answered her in much the same tone. She pulled up beside his car parked near the restaurant, where the evening had started off so promisingly, but their goodbyes were the cold, polite farewells of virtual strangers.

Chapter Sixteen

KATE SAT DOWN AT HER desk the next morning with a notebook full of scribbled memos, all of which seemed equally important. She started with Keith Doherty, checking back that his was the name that she'd seen on the victim statement from Tina Fetterdon. She hadn't been mistaken – he'd been the investigating officer on that case. Kate put the report down slowly, thinking. Then she brought up a search engine on her computer and typed in *Kevin Doherty*, along with various combinations such as *police officer, scandal, death*. She soon found the newspaper reports of his dismissal from the Abbeyford force and read through each link with increasing concentration. Detective Sergeant Kevin Doherty had been accused of sexual involvement with a female suspect in a burglary case. The case had eventually collapsed due to the unreliability of several key witnesses but, by that time, Doherty had already been dismissed from the force.

Kate re-read that part. He'd been dismissed,

not resigned. She looked at the photographs accompanying the article. Doherty had been a big man, bull-necked and thick shouldered. He looked like a dangerous thug, which, from reading between the lines, he probably had been. She searched again for articles on his untimely death, of which she also found plenty. Doherty had been found dead by the side of a lonely country road in the early morning of a Saturday in October, nineteen eighty. His injuries were consistent with being hit by a car but despite an investigation, no suspect was ever charged with his killing. Kate read through several more reports, noting that Doherty had also been linked to some rather dubious people, most notably a well-known criminal gang operating from Bristol at that time.

Kate looked at the photograph of the road where Doherty's body had been found; a small country road overlooked only by fields and hedges. Had he been run down deliberately? Or was it a genuine accident? Kate didn't suppose she would ever find out. Did his death have anything at all to do with the Marhaven care home or was it because of his involvement with another crime?

She sat back, easing the stiffness in her neck that came from reading hunched forward over the keyboard– so much for setting a good example for Theo – and looked up to see Anderton waving at her through the corridor window. She got up and made her way over to him.

"Just thought I'd let you know that I dropped in on Norman Chambers last night," Anderton said, as they got to his office. He gestured to Kate to take a seat and shut the door. "I was over that way anyway so I thought I might as well kill two birds with one stone."

He sat down in his chair, facing Kate over the desk. "Yes?" asked Kate. "Did he have anything to say about the two reports?"

Anderton tousled his hair for a moment. Then he sat forward, clasping both of his hands together. "I have to say that he didn't, really," he said. "It's not very surprising, it was so long ago. But he did promise to have a think and to see if he could recall anything about the girls and anything else that might help."

It was no more than Kate had expected but she was aware of a jab of disappointment. She murmured her thanks and went to get up – and then sat back down again. "Actually, if there is a chance to speak to him again, I'd like to know if he could tell me anything about Kevin Doherty."

Anderton's brows drew together. "Kevin Doherty? Now, why on Earth would you want to know about him?"

"You knew him?" asked Kate.

"Unfortunately, yes. We worked together on the same team for a few years – that's when Norman was my SO. He was for both of us. Doherty was... Well, let's just say *you* wouldn't have liked him."

Kate raised her eyebrows. "It doesn't sound much like you did either."

"I didn't," said Anderton. He sat back again in his seat. "He was a bigoted idiot with some very questionable views towards women. Getting rid of him was the best thing Abbeyford ever did."

Kate nodded. "So what do you think happened? His death, I mean."

Now it was Anderton's turn to raise his eyebrows. "Incredibly suspicious, I'd say. He was a man who liked to keep his friends close and his enemies closer. Perhaps they were one and the same, in this case."

"Right." Kate was silent for a moment, thinking. She was just opening her mouth to ask another question when Anderton said, "Anyway, Kate, I just thought I'd bring you up to speed. I'll let you know if I manage to speak to Norman again or if he has anything that can help us."

Kate knew a dismissal when she heard one. She gave her thanks again and got up.

"Oh, I'll be doing a debrief later," Anderton said just as she was leaving. "Warn the troops, will you? About three o'clock." Kate nodded. "Good stuff. I'll see you later."

Kate went back to her desk. Files and folders seemed to have bred in the short time she'd been away. Sighing, she tried to shuffle them into some sort of order, noting that there were at least three new cases vying for her attention. She flicked through them quickly. A sexual assault, a robbery, a suspicious death. Her gaze went to the fat folder on Jean Tripp. There were only so many hours in the day, and how many of them could she devote to this one case anymore? Sighing again, she pulled her chair up to her desk, picked up her pen, and got back to work.

She'd almost forgotten about Anderton's debrief that afternoon and had entirely failed to warn anyone that he'd be doing that, so it was lucky that all the team were coincidentally in the office when their boss came crashing in in his usual inimitable style. Kate waved frantically to Olbeck to attract his attention, guiltily aware that she'd forgotten to warn even him.

"Afternoon, team," Anderton said. "Just a quick update on where we are. Now, I know that most of you have been working very hard on the Munford Gorge case, and you've done well with it so far. But time is ticking on and the high-ups have just let me know that as from today, we'll be scaling back our time on that particular case. We're not closing it, don't get me wrong, but we're being snowed under with other work and I need to reallocate some resources."

Kate was aware of the faint feeling of surprise in the room, emanating from the others, as they digested what Anderton was saying. It wasn't the first time that investigations had been abruptly scaled down – there were only so many people and so much money, after all – but it hadn't happened for a while. Surprise was too mild a word for what Kate was feeling. Shock would have been a better choice of description. He's lying, she thought to herself, and was shocked again at the thought. *Why are we* really *pulling back on this case?*

Anderton was still talking, taking the team through the workload up ahead with the new cases that had come in. Theo and Jane were directed to the sexual assault case, with Fliss and Kate working with Olbeck on the others. Kate scarcely heard him. She was wondering what exactly she was going to ask once he'd stopped talking. How could she openly question his judgement without, well, questioning his judgement?

Anderton paused for breath and Kate shot her arm up into the air. "Yes, Kate?" asked Anderton and she could have sworn there was a tiny undercurrent of resignation in his voice, as if he'd been expecting her to make a fuss.

"What's going to happen with the Jean Tripp case? Sir," she added, after a moment.

"Management want it moved to Cold Cases. I should say that they've been asking for this for a while now and so far I've resisted."

"But you agree with them now?"

Anderton met her gaze steadily. "Yes, Kate, I do.

We're being flooded with other cases just as much in need of our attention – probably *more* in need of our attention."

Kate lowered her arm, unhappy with the answer but knowing this was not the time to start arguing. She let the others ask questions and Anderton answer them, all the while drumming her fingers moodily on the edge of her chair.

Eventually, the debrief was over, and people began to move back towards their work. Kate waited until Anderton had waved a hand in farewell and begun to walk back towards his office. She hurried after him but was briefly detained by running into Theo, who was moving with determination towards the coffee machine. Once they'd untangled themselves – *sorry, sorry mate, after you* – Kate walked as fast as she could towards Anderton's office. The door was firmly shut and Kate knew as well as anyone that that meant Anderton was not to be disturbed. She bit her lip, shifting from foot to foot outside the door. To hell with it. She raised her hand and knocked.

"What is it?" Anderton asked, once she'd peered around the door in answer to his "Come on in then, Kate. If you must." How had he known it was her?

"What's going on?" was what she asked, once she was inside with the door shut behind her.

"What do you mean?"

"You know what I mean." This was skirting

dangerously close to being disrespectful but at the moment, Kate was angry enough not to care. "Why the hurry to close this case?"

"We're not *closing* it, like I said. It's moving to Cold Cases. It's no longer top priority, that's all."

Kate sat down with a thud. "Why's it not top priority?"

"Oh, Kate." Anderton sighed. "Because this department doesn't have an unlimited personnel budget? Because we don't have an unlimited budget, full stop? Because I've got cases queuing up that involve people suffering here and now, not forty years in the past? That enough for you?"

Kate bit her lip. "We were making good progress—"

"I know that," Anderton interrupted, but in a gentler tone. "Your hard work hasn't gone unnoticed, believe me. I know you like to see things through to the bitter end but believe me, Kate, sometimes the decision is just out of my hands. I'm sorry."

"But—" protested Kate, unsure of what else she could say.

"Kate," said Anderton with finality. "I understand your disappointment but it's out of my hands. I need you to get started on the new cases, right now. Can I ask you to do that?"

Kate swallowed down her annoyance. "Yes, sir," she muttered, after a moment of seething silence.

"Good." Anderton looked down at his cluttered desk and sighed. "Was that all?"

"*Yes*," said Kate, trying to infuse that one word with all her anger and resentment. She wasn't sure it had worked.

"Right. Off you go then."

Kate walked back to her desk, doing her best not to stamp. She flung herself into her chair, clicking her mouse moodily. What the hell was wrong with Anderton? She tried telling herself it was nothing, going over all the reasons he'd given her for the reallocation of the case, but it didn't work. The same phrase repeated itself again and again in her head. *He's lying. He's lying.*

"Cup of tea, Kate?"

Kate barely heard Fliss's offer. When it was repeated, she looked up and muttered something, a yes, a no, she didn't really care. The file for the new case was already on her desk, placed on top of the bulging folder that contained all of Kate's work on the Jean Tripp case. Kate looked at the new folder and then pushed it aside, petulantly. Then she took the Jean Tripp file and walked over to the storage room with it.

"Sorry, Jean," she muttered as she locked the file away in the cabinet. What was Anderton's phrase? "It's out of my hands."

She heard her mobile ringing as she was walking back to her desk and ran to answer it. It was Jay.

"What's up?"

"It's Mum." Kate's heart gave a massive thump but Jay was already speaking as if he could hear her reaction. "Listen, don't panic, don't worry, but you know she's been in hospital?"

"Yes – I was going to visit her." Kate was conscious of a spurt of guilt, realising she hadn't even bothered to find out which hospital Mary had actually been admitted to.

"Well, they've moved her out of there into some sort of hospice. They didn't say as much but I think she's taken a turn for the worse. Me and Laura are going down there tomorrow to see her. Will you come too?"

Kate suddenly realised she was standing stock still in the middle of the office floor. People were looking at her with concern. Turning away and heading for the corridor, she said "Yes. Yes, of course. Where is it?"

Jay named a suburb on the outskirts of Bournemouth. Kate agreed to meet them there tomorrow at eleven, adding "Can you text me the details, Jay? I haven't got a pen on me." She felt so flustered and upset she knew there was no hope of her mind retaining the details.

They said goodbye and she trailed back to her desk, slumping down in her seat. She could see Fliss giving her worried looks across the table and straightened up, wanting to deflect any questions.

She reached for the folder on the new case, opened it and began to read, but the words could have been in an unknown language for all the sense they made.

Mum's dying. That was the first time that Kate had truly taken it in. *She's dying.* She could feel her eyes begin to burn and, not wanting to cry at her desk, jumped up and hurried for the ladies', where at least she could sob in a modicum of peace.

When she got home that evening, the first thing she did was to pick Merlin up and bury her face in his soft black fur. She sat down on the sofa, hugging him against her until he squirmed out of her tight grip and ran away towards the kitchen. "Stupid cat," muttered Kate. In a minute, she would get up and feed him, would start to think about making dinner, would hang out the washing and take the rubbish out – all the chores that kept the house running – but just at that very moment, all she could do was lie on the sofa and stare up at the ceiling, thinking of her mum and of Jean and of what the hell she was going to do.

Chapter Seventeen

THE BAD WEATHER FINALLY BROKE the next day. Kate drove along the motorway in a blaze of spring sunshine. She could see patches of snowdrops on the banks of the dual carriageway with a cheerful burst of yellow daffodils here and there. Perhaps Jeff and Mark would have sunshine on their wedding day, she thought sentimentally and then cursed as she realised she still hadn't done that bloody speech. Tonight, I'll do it tonight, she promised herself, knowing full well that she would probably forget again.

The hospice where Mary Redman was staying was a modern brick building, set in some landscaped grounds, all one storey. Kate assumed that was to make it easier for patients to be transported around; no worries with stairs and falls if everything was on the ground floor. She saw Jay and Laura getting out of their car as she pulled into the car park and waved, feeling a burst of happiness at the sight of her brother that not even the anticipation of the grimness of this particular visit could dim.

"You're looking well," she said to Laura as they walked towards the entrance.

"You're looking knackered," said Jay, peering at her face. "Are you working too hard?"

Kate couldn't help but laugh. "When aren't I working too hard? You know how it is."

They made their way inside the building. Directed by the woman at the reception desk, they found Mary's room quite easily. Jay knocked and they all heard Mary's breathless voice telling them to come in.

As shocked as Kate had been by the first sight of her mother, all those weeks ago, that was nothing to the shock she felt now, looking at the woman who lay on the bed before her. Mary was skeletally thin, the bones of her skull protruding from the almost translucent skin that overlaid them. She lay almost lost in the hospital sheets, wearing a cotton nightgown that echoed the colour of her skin; white, with an undertone of grey. Mary still wore her coppery wig, and there was something so brave and yet so pathetic about the sight that Kate felt her throat closing up. Blinking, she followed Jay and Laura's example and kissed her mother hello, trying not to tighten up her face as their cheeks made contact.

She let Jay and Laura do most of the talking, finding herself a seat that was furthest from the bed. Laura asked some gentle, appropriate questions about how Mary was feeling, like the thoughtful, considerate girl that she was. Kate sat back and listened, letting her eyes roam about the room. It was quite a nice room, the walls painted in a peaceful grey-blue, a framed painting of an impressionist print over on the far wall. The owners of the hospice had obviously tried to make it seem as little like a hospital room as possible, but you couldn't escape the oxygen tanks, the medication on the side table by the bed, and the bed itself, which could be raised or lowered as needed. An oxygen mask lay beside Mary's limp hand and every so often she would lift it to her face and gasp weakly.

At last, Jay and Laura began to make tentative noises about leaving, and Kate jumped up, trying not to appear too eager to leave. Again, she kissed her mother's cheek and said something cheerful and fatuous about being back soon and was at the door when her mother said, in the strongest voice that Kate had heard today, "Kelly. Wait."

Jay and Laura turned enquiringly to Kate. She herself turned back to her mother, eyebrows raised, hoping she didn't appear too impatient. "What's wrong, Mum?"

Mary took a gasp of oxygen. "I want to speak to Kelly – to Kate – alone."

Kate sighed inwardly. "It's okay, I'll see you guys later," she said. "Don't wait for me." After exchanging hugs with them both, she saw them both out of the door and then returned to the bed, trying to keep her face neutral. "What is it, Mum?"

She was bracing herself for a bollocking, a diatribe on her real or imagined failings, although she couldn't quite pinpoint what it was Mary thought she'd done. It was just the low-level, permanent miasma of guilt she carried about with her, that's what it was. Kate sat down again, this time nearer to the bed.

Mary looked at her from over the black rubber rim of the mask, the clear part of the plastic clogged with spittle. Kate looked into her mother's eyes. What she saw surprised her. There was no anger there, but there was an unmistakeable appeal. "What do you want, Mum?" she asked again, more gently.

Mary tore the mask from her face. "I want to make a statement," she said, once she was able to talk again. "I want to make a statement about my time at Marhaven and what happened."

Kate's heart thumped. "About Marhaven."

Mary nodded, struggling either for breath or through the grip of strong emotion. "I've not got much time left, but I need to do it. It's important. They shouldn't get away with it, it's been too many years but we can put it right, Kelly, you and me. But you've got to help me."

Kate leant forward and took her mother's bony hand. "I'll help you. Just tell me why you want to do this now?"

Mary gave a hoarse cough and Kate flinched back a little until she realised that her mother was trying to laugh. "'Cos I'm *dying*, Kelly, aren't I? I want to set things right before I go. God knows I was always a useless bloody mother, but this is my chance to do something right for a change. I want to make a statement, I need to tell someone what happened at Marhaven. As much as I know."

"Okay," said Kate, "That's no problem. We can—"

Mary interrupted her, both in voice and with a hand that clutched back at hers with desperate strength. "I can't tell you everything but there were others there. They'll tell you too, once I've got things started. That's how it always works, doesn't it, other girls come forward. There was two, two who knew stuff that went on. Sarah, that was one of them. Talk to Sarah. Tell her to be brave and tell someone too." Mary coughed and fastened the mask to her face. Kate stared at her as she gasped in the oxygen, willing her to be able to carry on. At last, Mary pulled the mask away from her face. "Sarah always said she was a warrior. Said she wanted to be that one, the one who fought the Romans, the woman chief."

"Boudicca?" asked Kate, doubtfully.

"That's it. Tell Sarah to be Boudicca. It's not too late. Tin'll help you if you ask him. But I need to make my statement, and soon, Kelly – Kate."

Transfixed by her mother's gaze, Kate nodded slowly. "I can't take it myself, Mum," she said. "But there's several people at work who can do it. I'll get one of them down here tomorrow. They've been trained for it, for this kind of thing. Tomorrow, you have my word."

Mary nodded. She held the mask up to her face again briefly before seeming to shrink back on the pillows. Her eyelids fluttered. "I'm tired," she said after a moment. "Worn me out, that has. You go now, Kelly. Go and sort it out for me."

"Yes. Yes, I will. Try and rest now, Mum. I'll have an officer here first thing tomorrow to talk to you and you can take all the time in the world."

Mary smiled. Her eyes closed and she murmured something, so that Kate had to lean in to hear. "That's what I haven't got."

"Well..." Kate stood up, preparing to go. Then she leant down and hugged her mother, properly, feeling the bones of her mother's chest and shoulders beneath her arms. "Well done, Mum," she said, equally as quietly. "We'll sort it out together."

"Good girl." Mary turned her head and fastened the mask back onto her face, dismissing her. Kate looked at her for a long moment and then left, shutting the door gently behind her.

Chapter Eighteen

THE SECOND THING THAT KATE did the next morning on reaching the office was to call her mother. Unable to reach her by mobile phone, Kate redialled the hospice reception and informed them that someone from Abbeyford Police Station would be arriving that morning to take a victim statement from her mother. She gave the details of her colleague, Jane, to the receptionist, hearing the undercurrent of surprise and curiousity running beneath the receptionist's usual bland tones. Finally, she asked if her mother could call her back when she was able – if she was able to – and said goodbye.

Right. One job done and ticked off the list. Kate jumped up and headed for the file storage room. She planned to look through the Jean Tripp file once more, to cross-check against what her mother had told her. Surely there must be another lead there, something that might bring this case forward, back into the remit of Kate's team?

The Abbeyford CID team kept their case files in a secure room, able to be entered only through a door protected by a key code. Kate punched it in and pushed at the heavy door. The room beyond was small and windowless and always slightly too warm (it was amazing how much overdue filing got done on cold winter days). Kate went to the filing cabinet, slid the drawer out with a metallic clang and then stopped dead.

The file was missing.

She could see that straight away, the emptiness of the cardboard hanging file which had held the manila folder. She could see that, but still she searched the files before and after it, right to the end of the drawer. Then she slid out the one below and searched that, and then the final drawer nearest the floor. Nothing.

Kate slowly slid the metal drawers back into the cabinet. She was aware of her heart beating just that little bit faster. Don't panic, she told herself. Chances are it's already gone down to Cold Cases. Don't panic – yet.

She shut the door of the storage room firmly behind her and walked over to Theo's desk.

"Um, did anyone from CC come up and get the Jean Tripp file yet? That you know of?" she asked, in as casual a tone as possible.

Theo looked up from his report. "Nope. Don't think so." He shouted Fliss's name across the room.

186

"Fliss! Anyone come up to collect that Jean Tripp file?"

Fliss was shaking her head. "No. No one. Why?"

"Oh, doesn't matter," said Kate, trying to smile. "It's not important."

"Because they wouldn't have the codes to the storage room without asking us, would they?" asked Fliss. She got up then and moved closer. "Is something wrong?"

She was clearly worried that she was in trouble for something. Kate forced herself to smile properly and say, "No, no, don't worry. I think I know where it is, anyway. Seriously, Fliss, it's fine."

Mollified, Fliss took herself back to her desk. Kate sat down opposite her, trying to breathe and act normally. The office hummed about her in its usual state – telephones ringing, photocopiers whirring, people talking – the normal, everyday sounds of a workplace. But Kate couldn't relax, couldn't stop thinking about what the missing file might mean. She knew she had put it there the night before last, she knew it. Stop panicking, she instructed herself once more. Olbeck's probably got it – or Anderton.

At the thought of Anderton, her heart gave another great thump. There *had* been something odd about him, she couldn't escape that. Why had he shut the investigation down so suddenly? Kate hunched forward, her forehead propped against her hand as she stared down at the surface of her desk, thinking. Could he have taken the file? Why?

She jumped up again and made her way over to Olbeck's empty office. She marched in purposefully and took a quick scan of his desk, the top of his filing cabinet, the pile of files on the carpet. Nothing there that looked like the Tripp file. Where was he, anyway? She suddenly realised he had the morning off – more wedding stuff with Jeff, no doubt. Should she call him and see if he had the file? But how could he, when any file that had to be taken out of the office had to be logged and signed out and there was nothing in the log book for the Jean Tripp file since last night?

All right then. Kate took a deep breath and went to Anderton's office. The blinds were down and the door closed but she knocked anyway, holding her breath for the sound of his voice curtly telling her to come in. There was nothing but silence. Kate hesitated for a moment. Then, looking up and down the corridor and seeing that no one was in sight, she opened the door to Anderton's office and quickly slipped inside, shutting it behind her.

I'm just having a look, she told herself, heart thumping once more. She checked the surface of his desk, looked underneath – nothing there but a large black gym bag – and quickly scanned the rest of the room. She couldn't see it anywhere. Biting her lip, Kate listened out once more. Hearing nothing, she took a quick, guilty glance at the door and then, before she lost her nerve, opened the drawers to his desk one by one.

If anyone caught her doing this, she would be in so much trouble it wasn't funny. *Stop this, stop this*, she screamed at herself, but somehow she was still doing it, still searching through the cupboards and filing cabinets, blood pounding in her ears. She was holding her breath but even over the thump of her heartbeat, she became aware of the sound of footfalls in the corridor outside, growing louder. Almost slipping in her haste, Kate dashed back round to the other side of Anderton's desk and flung herself in a chair, just as the door handle clicked and the door opened.

"Kate," said Anderton a moment later, surprised by the sight of her. Kate pinned a smile on her face. She hoped she wasn't too obviously red-faced. "What can I do for you?"

Kate's mind went blank. She groped for a second. "I just wanted to know if you had five minutes. Not now. Later," she added, terrified that he'd ask her to tell him all about whatever was bothering her that very moment.

"What about?"

Again, Kate's mind went blank. "Um – um – I'd rather not go into it right now," she said after a moment. She unconsciously wiped her sweating palms on the sides of her thighs. "If that's okay. I'll bring you up to speed fully later."

Anderton was looking at her slightly oddly.

"Okay," he said in a voice that didn't sound too convinced. "I'll give you a shout when I'm free."

"Great," Kate said, overcompensating. She fought down a blush. "I'll be around. Thanks. Thanks very much."

She scuttled back to her desk and collapsed in her chair. What the hell was going on? She tried to think back to whether a file had ever been lost before. It must have happened, human error was always a possibility but...

After a moment, Kate got up and went back to the storage room. While she was waiting for Anderton, she decided to go through every cabinet in that room – just in case.

It was getting on for six o'clock when Anderton finally reappeared. Kate sat at her desk, staring blankly at her computer screen. Across from her, Fliss was chatting continuously about her plans for the evening, about one word in ten of which was penetrating Kate's consciousness.

"Kate." Anderton appeared behind her shoulder with suddenness, making her jump. "When you're ready, I am."

Kate got up and made to follow him. He shook his head minutely at her and leant forward, close enough to whisper something before moving away, heading back out of the office door. Kate stared after him. Had he just said 'get your stuff'?

Heart beginning to speed up a little, Kate

gathered her coat and bag, said goodbye to Fliss in a mutter and hurried out. She nearly ran straight into Anderton who was waiting for her in the corridor.

"My car. Come on. Right now."

What the hell? Kate hurried after her boss, bag slipping in her sweating hands. Oh God, was she about to be fired? Had he seen her searching his room? Swallowing hard, Kate almost ran after his swiftly striding figure, hurrying behind him down the stairs and through the echoing metal doors to the underground car park, all the way over to Anderton's car, parked at the far edge of the grounds.

Kate was buckled in and they were speeding away from the station before Anderton spoke.

"Sorry about that... abruptness. I thought we'd go for a drink. That okay with you?"

"Sure," said Kate, so worried and confused she hardly heard herself. What the hell was going on? She was driven inescapably back to that time, years ago now, when she and Anderton had had a one night stand. Was this – was this – did he mean to finally make a move? Not *now*, surely? Oh God, it can't be that, thought Kate. I'm in trouble here, big trouble. She said nothing else for the duration of the drive, waiting and worrying until Anderton drew into the car park of a pub unknown to Kate.

Inside the pub, it was nice – open fires and fairy lights strung along the wainscoting, a decent countryside sort of pub. Anderton ushered Kate through the building to a little snug at the back, where there was only room for one settle and a table.

"Bit easier to talk here," said Anderton. Kate subsided on to the seat feeling as if she were trapped in some kind of dream. "What will you have?"

While he was at the bar, Kate tried to collect herself. Don't admit to anything, don't do anything rash, she told herself, wishing she felt calmer. She thought of Magda and the breathing exercises she'd taught her and tried to do some of the more unobtrusive ones, stopping as Anderton came back into the little room with their drinks.

"Now," he said, sitting back down and taking a hearty pull of his pint. "Sorry about all that cloak and dagger stuff."

Kate gathered her courage. "What's going on?"

Anderton looked into the golden depths of his drink for a moment. "Has it struck you – do you think that there's something a bit funny going on at work?"

What exactly did he mean? Kate wavered for a moment and then bit the bullet. "Yes," she said bluntly. "I do. For a start—" she stared him straight in the eye. "The Jean Tripp file has gone missing."

"No, it hasn't."

Kate was almost winded. "What? Yes it has. I looked for it everywhere today, nobody's seen it, nobody's logged it out—"

"It's not missing. Or if it is, it's gone missing in my gym bag."

Kate thought for a moment she'd misheard. "What?"

"Shh," Anderton said, leaning in a little closer. "I said, I've got it."

Kate's eyes bulged. "You have? Why?"

Anderton sat back again and took a gulp of beer. "Because I didn't want it to go missing *permanently*," he said, putting his glass back down again.

Kate drew a breath in through her nostrils. "Okay," she said, after she'd calmed down a little. "What's going on?"

Anderton leant forward again. "Something bloody odd is going on, that's what I think," he said quietly. "That's why I wanted to come here, so we couldn't be overheard. Something definitely dodgy is going on."

"So, what?" Kate asked, equally quietly.

"I've thought it ever since I went to see Norman. He didn't seem that surprised to be asked the questions that I asked him. Now, why would that be, seeing as the events I was asking him about happened almost forty years ago?" Anderton glanced around as if expecting to see someone eavesdropping. "He was – he was as normal as he could be but – I don't know – there was something. He was lying to me, about something."

Kate slumped a little in her seat, almost weak with relief. There she had been, thinking that Anderton had been the one putting the spoke in the wheels, trying to shut down the investigation when that wasn't the case at all. Although... she felt a sudden jump of paranoia. Had he purposefully asked her here and told her this in order to keep her on side?

"When I asked you about Kevin Doherty," she began, cautiously. "You were the same. You didn't even ask me why I wanted to know about him, someone that you can't have even thought of for decades."

"That's why," Anderton said grimly. "I'd already started to get suspicious. I went to question Norman, question him about something that should have been quite innocuous. A couple of days later, I'm told that I'm to shunt the case over to Cold Cases, it's not top priority anymore. You can imagine that didn't sit well with me."

"You still did it though," Kate said, resentment still present in her tone.

Anderton gave her a look. "Kate, believe me, I had no choice. Besides..." He lowered his voice. "If you're thinking what I'm thinking, then the worst thing to do is start hurling accusations around before we've even got any evidence."

Kate then took a look around the empty little snug herself. "What are we thinking?" she murmured.

Anderton took another bracing pull of his pint. The glass was almost empty and Kate spared a thought, a minor worry, about how she was going to get back home. "We're being told not to take an interest, in so many words," Anderton said. "I don't like that. That doesn't sit well with me. There were always rumours about Doherty but nothing – nothing concrete. He was a dodgy bugger, though. What if he had something to do with this case? That's corruption at the highest level, Kate. Cover ups. Whitewashing. We've seen it happen recently, in Rotherham, with Savile. All those people who let those things happen or turned a blind eye."

Kate was hanging onto every word, almost breathless. The momentary paranoia she'd had, that Anderton was just out to trip her up, dissipated. Sincerity rang in his every word. "So, what do we do?" she asked.

Anderton sighed. "I need another drink for this."

Kate folded her lips together for a moment. I can always get a cab, she thought and got up, offering to get them this time.

She ducked back into the corridor that led back to the main bar. Waiting there, she felt a blast of cold air as, behind her, the door to the road opened. Kate looked into the mirror that ran the length of the bar and straight into the reflected eyes of Fliss, who had crowded into the pub with what looked like about ten other girls.

Fliss saw her and immediately smiled and waved. Kate, after a moment, did the same. She didn't turn, but saw Fliss approaching her in the mirror, and only as she saw her arrive just behind her did she swing round.

"Hi, Kate," said Fliss. "What a coincidence! We're having a bit of a pub crawl. Want to join us or are you here with someone?"

"I'm – well, I'm—" began Kate before, to her horror, she saw Anderton appear in the corridor doorway to the bar. Too late, she drew her gaze back from him as if he were red hot, but not before Fliss had looked herself and seen him.

"Oh!" Kate heard the exclamation and cringed. Then Anderton was coming over, smooth as you like, hailing Fliss and chastising Kate for the lateness of their drinks order.

He, Fliss and Kate chatted for a few excruciating minutes before Fliss excused herself and with a rather strained 'goodbye' and left to go and join her friends who were gathered in a noisy circle in the corner of the main room of the pub. Kate and Anderton took their drinks back to the snug in silence.

"Well," said Kate, unable to help herself, as they sat back down. "That's torn it."

"Oh, don't worry about it," said Anderton, breezily. "She'll just think we're having an affair," he added, causing Kate to spit her drink out across the table.

"Bloody hell," said Kate, as they mopped up. "Sorry. But, honestly."

"Seriously, don't worry about it. We've got

more important things to worry about." Anderton pushed the little pile of soggy paper napkins to the side of the table and folded his hands on the table. "So, this is what I was going to suggest. Do some investigating on your own. Take some time off and go and see what you can dig up." He caught sight of her face. "What's the matter? Not keen?"

"It's not that," said Kate. "I'm just as keen to see this one through as you are. But why—" She hesitated for a moment. "Why can't we do it officially? Blow the whole thing open and start another investigation?"

Anderton didn't reply for a moment. "We don't have the evidence," he said eventually.

"Oh, come on," Kate said. "We've got a dead body, a statement from someone who was at Marhaven with the victim, we've got the names of the other girls who were there." She stopped, wondering whether she should mention Tom Marks and his story. "What's stopping us?"

Anderton sighed. "Kate, it's – it's difficult. Take it from me, they wouldn't make it easy. It could be a big mistake to go any further officially without some *serious* evidence."

Kate eyed her boss for a long moment, conscious of a sinking feeling in her stomach. "Why won't you do it?" she demanded after a moment. "What's the real reason?"

"I've told you."

Kate scoffed. Then, as realisation dawned, she said, unable to stop her lip curling. "Oh. *I* see."

"What?"

Kate folded her arms. "What have they got on you?"

"I don't know what you mean."

"No?" Kate tried to keep the anger out of her voice and failed. "What have you done that gives them such a hold over you?"

Their eyes met for a long, charged moment. Then Anderton broke the contact, looking down at the table. "This isn't to go any further."

Kate rolled her eyes. "Naturally."

There was an edge to Anderton's voice. "Nobody's perfect, Kate. Not even you." Their eyes met again and this time Kate flushed, partly from anger, partly from memory of their brief affair. Anderton went on, looking away. "I – I slept with a suspect. She – she didn't take kindly to me breaking it off once I realised what a stupid thing it was I was doing. Made a complaint against me. It was dropped for lack of evidence but – it's still there, in the records. It could make life very difficult for me if, *by some coincidence*, it was made public knowledge."

Kate stared at him. "Does any of this sound familiar? What were we just talking about?"

"Exactly!" Anderton leant forward again. "That's why I think there's a cover-up going on. Someone has something on someone very senior. That's why we can't let this lie, Kate, as much as they want us to. But I'm not risking my job without being damn sure of a conviction. I'm sorry, but that's that. No arguments."

For a moment, Kate thought about protesting. But she could see the sense in what he was saying. If Anderton's seniority wouldn't be enough to save him, then where did that leave her? Out in the cold, that was where. Slowly, she nodded.

"Good," said Anderton. "Now, drink up and I'll drop you home. Don't look like that—" He added, seeing Kate's significant glance at his empty glass. "I've only had two pints. Now, I'll sign you off on holiday from tomorrow. See what you can dig up. Didn't you say your mother had made a statement?" Kate nodded. "Great. That's a good start. Plan your action and keep me posted."

Kate threw him an ironic salute. "Aye-aye, captain."

Anderton smiled and for one moment, there was just the slightest hint of the possibility of something more between them. Kate turned her face sharply away, breaking their gaze. Don't start that again, she told herself. They walked towards the exit of the pub and Anderton and Kate both waved to Fliss, who returned it rather uncertainly. Kate worried about how she was going to handle the inevitable questions at work tomorrow before realising that she wouldn't be there and her spirits lightened. On the way home she sent a text to Tin apologising for her silence and asking him just one question. Then she put the phone away, answered Anderton's small talk as best she could and inwardly, made her plans.

Chapter Nineteen

"THANKS FOR COMING," SAID KATE, glancing over at her passenger.

"Humph," said Tin, sounding a little cool. "I surprise myself, sometimes."

Kate glanced over at him once more and was relieved to find that he was half-smiling. She faced the road again and checked the sat nav. Half an hour until they would reach their destination.

"So, tell me as much as you can about Sarah Smith," she said. "I know she lives in Haworth, that she was at Marhaven, that she was one of the girls who accused Godfrey Peters of sexual assault. What happened to her after that?"

Tin leant his head back against the head rest. "She left the country," he said. "Not long after she made that accusation."

"Seriously?" Kate raised her eyebrows. "But she was – wasn't she underage? Although—" She considered for a moment. "If she'd travelled with someone, an older person for example, that might not have flagged up any concern."

"Exactly," said Tin. "She was reported missing by the Marhaven home not long after that accusation was made. No one was really concerned – she was a habitual runaway, a troubled, argumentative little madam, according to those who remember her. Anyway, I managed to trace her movements into Spain, then I think she went to Australia and was out there for years. She only came back to the UK a few years ago."

"Have you managed to talk to her before?"

Tin shook his head. "Wouldn't even open the door to me. I had the devil's own job trying to actually find her here. She must have changed her name more than once, got married maybe."

Something that Tin had said had rung a faint bell with Kate. She frowned, trying to pinpoint what it was, but it slipped away from her. Never mind. It would come back.

They were approaching Haworth now. The drive had been a pleasant one, winding their way through the calm, green hills of the Yorkshire dales, the grassy flanks of the hills criss-crossed with the grey lines of the drystone walls and dotted here and there with grubby looking sheep. Kate drew the car into a layby for a moment at the top of the road into the town and they looked down at the valley, the stone cottages and winding streets, and up on the opposite hill, the building made famous as the home of the Bronte sisters. Kate felt a fleeting disappointment that they wouldn't have time to go and have a closer look.

"You're sure that's her address?" she asked Tin.

"Unless she's moved in the two months since I tried to talk to her."

"Okay." Kate put the car in gear and pulled back onto the road. "Let's do this."

The street on which Sarah Smith lived was a typical one: rows of little stone cottages with doors opening directly on to the cobbled streets. Kate found a parking space at the end of the road and shut off the engine.

"Shall we both go?" she asked Tin.

"Not to start. Let me try again. I can tell her that things have moved on in the investigation. Talk to her about Jean Tripp. That might work."

Kate nodded slowly. "Okay. If you don't get anywhere, come back and I'll have a go."

She watched Tin walk towards the house in her rear-view mirror and was momentarily side-tracked in admiring his rear view. Recollecting herself, she put the time to good use in trying to find them both somewhere to stay for the night. She found a likely looking hotel, made the booking there and then and was just trying to check her emails when the car door opened and made her jump.

Tin got in, grim-faced. "Nothing. She won't even open the door."

"But she's in?"

"Yes. I saw the curtains move in the front room."

Kate considered. "All right. Leave it for now. I've found us a hotel, so let's check in and we'll come back after lunch." She thought, but didn't add, *if she continues to refuse, I'm pulling out my warrant card*. Hopefully it wouldn't come to that.

The hotel actually turned out to be a local pub, the accommodation rather basic but at least clean and comfortable. Kate had hesitated but in the end had booked two rooms adjoining one another. She was starting to think that her fledgling relationship with Tin had crossed the line from romance to business-like friendship. I'm not going to worry about that now, she reminded herself. Keep your mind on the job, Kate.

They had lunch in the pub. Kate could see Tin attracting some curious but not hostile glances from the locals at the bar and felt cross for him. He was eating his steak and kidney pie, seemingly oblivious to the attention, and after a moment Kate shrugged off her anger and turned her attention to the excellent food.

After coffee, the two of them faced each other across the table.

"We're trying again?" asked Tin.

Kate nodded. "It's my turn now," she added, as they made their way to the door.

Sarah Smith lived behind a door that was covered in peeling red paint, as if the wood was afflicted with some kind of skin disease. Kate knocked using the dull metal knocker, rang the doorbell, knocked again. Nothing. She leant forward, almost certain she could hear the woman breathing, standing behind that implacable door like a statue.

"Ms. Smith," Kate called, as quietly as she could but still hopefully loud enough to be heard. "Ms. Smith, don't be alarmed but I really need to speak with you. Can you hear me? Can you open this door?"

She did hear it then, a distinct intake of breath. Kate leant ever closer and carried on with her pleas. "Ms. Smith – Sarah – I need to talk to you. I don't mean you any harm, in fact, I'm here to help you. Can you let me in? Please?"

Nothing. Silence. Baulked, Kate stood back for a moment, cast a frustrated glance at Tin who was hovering several feet away and then leant back towards the door.

"Sarah, my name is Kate Redman. I'm a—" She stopped herself finishing the sentence. *I'm a police officer*. That would probably not help her case at all. Going blank for a moment, she then remembered. She leant forward again. "Sarah, I'm Kate Redman. I'm Mary Redman's daughter. She was with you in the Marhaven home in the seventies. Do you remember? I think you were friends. Mary Redman. She said I had to talk to you."

Nothing still. In increasing desperation, Kate pressed herself onto the peeling paint, ignoring the curious looks from passers-by. "Sarah," she said, her mouth at the keyhole. "Mary told me to talk to you. She said to be brave. She said to be Boudicca." Kate could feel the cold metal of the keyhole against her mouth. "Be Boudicca," she repeated, desperately.

There was a sudden click, as of a bolt drawing back. Kate drew back from the door, holding her breath. The door swung inwards by a few inches and Kate could see, framed in the gap, the face of Sarah Smith.

"Sarah?" she asked, tentatively. There was a small nod from the woman standing in the doorway.

"You can come in," said Sarah in a low voice, that still carried a slight Australian twang. Then, as Tin made a move towards the door, she pulled it back towards her until only an inch of space showed. "Not you. Just her."

"Go on," said Kate to Tin. She handed him the car keys. Then, as Sarah drew the door open again, just wide enough for Kate to slip through, she entered the house.

The door opened straight into the living room, as was customary with these old houses. The room was dark, curtains pulled against the daylight, and warm – the central heating was obviously on. Kate and Sarah stood silently regarding each other for a moment. Sarah was a tall, heavy woman, with rather beautiful thick, blonde hair. Crows-feet cut sharply into the skin around her brown eyes and her face was spattered with freckles.

"Wow," said Sarah after a moment. "You do really look like Mary. I haven't seen her in so many years but looking at you... Wow. It brings it all back."

Her face clouded. Moving further into the room, she turned back to Kate to ask a question. "Do you want a drink?"

"Tea would be lovely—" Kate began before realising that Sarah was reaching for a bottle of red wine that stood on the sideboard. "Oh, no thanks," she added hastily. "I'm fine."

"I don't normally drink during the day," said Sarah. "But I think I might need one now." Kate was reminded of Tom Marks. Sarah poured herself a generous glass and sat down on one of the two armchairs in the room. Kate sank back into the other, facing her.

There was a short silence whilst Sarah drank her wine. Kate studied her covertly. She probably hadn't ever been pretty but there was both strength and character in her face. No wedding ring. She was dressed in comfortable, drab clothes; loose grey tracksuit trousers and a baggy grey jumper. She was probably the same age as Mary Redman but she looked younger. That wasn't hard, Kate thought, feeling a pang at the thought of her mother.

As if Sarah had read her mind, she looked up. "Why does Mary want you to talk to me? All that stuff that happened was so long ago. Why does she think we can do anything about it now?"

Kate leant forward clasping her hands and wondering how to begin. In the end, she decided to tell the truth. "Mary – Mum – she's got terminal cancer. She's dying." Sarah said nothing but winced a little. "She's already given a statement to the police about what she saw at Marhaven, the sexual abuse allegations. She wants to bring it all to light before she – before she dies." Kate felt her throat close up at these words and stopped speaking abruptly.

Sarah hadn't taken her eyes off Kate's face. Something in her own face reflected Kate's anguish for a moment. "Mary was always brave. She's the one who taught me about Boudicca. She was sort of a heroine to us both. We needed a role model in that place, by God we did."

Kate cleared her throat. "So, tell me about it."

Sarah was silent. Then she jumped up and poured herself another glass of wine, a bigger one this time. Then she sat down again.

"It's all right," she said, catching Kate's glance at her brimming glass. "I won't have any more. I won't be drunk if that's what you're thinking." She took a sip, put the glass down on the coffee table in front of her, and sighed. "I haven't talked about this in years. I thought I'd almost managed to forget about

CELINA GRACE

it. I've had so much therapy, you wouldn't believe...
It did work, mostly. It got me through. I mean, I'm
still here, aren't I? Not like the other one who came
with me to the station, what was her name?"

"Tina Fetterden," said Kate.

"Yeah, her. Jesus, it took us such a lot of... I mean,
trying to get the courage up to report *him* and his
dirty little secrets. And then nothing ever happened.
I started getting worried though, especially after
Jonie said she was going to the papers—"

Kate didn't want to interrupt her but she had to.
"Who's 'him', Sarah?"

"Mr Peters. The guy who ran the home, him and
his weird sister."

Kate nodded. Sarah went on speaking, haltingly
but without stopping. "He was a paedophile. It was
the perfect job for him, wasn't it, in charge of all
these young girls, these young troubled vulnerable
girls, who nobody was going to believe when they
tried to tell someone about what he did. He used
to pimp us out, you know." Sarah looked up at Kate
through a curtain of blonde hair. "He used to lend
us out to all his rich and powerful friends. A taxi
would come and pick us up and take us to this hotel
in Bristol. The hotel owner was one of them, one
of the men. They'd give us drugs and alcohol and
take it in turns to rape us." She was shaking now,
what was left of the wine sloshing dangerously
in her glass. Gently Kate reached out and took it

from her, putting it down on the coffee table. Sarah carried on speaking. "There were all sorts of men there, doctors and lawyers and police. I should have known not to bother going to report him."

Kate's skin was prickling. "There was a police officer there? Did you know his name?"

Sarah clasped both of her hands together. "I didn't at first. Then Jonie found out. That's what she said she was going to tell the journalist she went to."

Kevin Doherty. Kate was dying to mention his name but she knew she mustn't lead the witness. "What was his name, Sarah?" she repeated, gently.

"I don't know his first name. But he was there all the time. Chambers, that was it. Someone Chambers."

For a second, Kate thought she'd misheard her. She swallowed. "Chambers?"

"Yeah. Him and that other copper used to come. The big one, he was awful. I thought he'd killed Tina once, he was so rough." Sarah looked down at her clasped hands. Kate thought she saw a tear fall from behind that blonde curtain of hair. "He had an Irish name, the big one. Kevin something."

Kate's heart was thumping so loudly she was surprised Sarah couldn't hear it. *Chambers*. She could feel her hands begin to shake. If Norman Chambers had been part of a paedophile ring... Kate ß

took a deep breath and then another. What the hell was she going to do now?

"Can you tell me anything more?" she asked Sarah, hoping her voice wasn't trembling too much.

Sarah unclasped her hands and wiped the palms along the sides of her tracksuit trouser, leaving a faint grey mark. "It started not long after we arrived at the home. He used to touch us, that Peters, and make us do things. He'd give us stuff afterwards, fags and sweets and stuff like that, but he made it pretty plain that nobody would believe us if we told anyone, and if we told anyone, we'd be out of Marhaven and then where would we go? We were in the last chance saloon there. I don't know why I didn't run away sooner, to be honest. I suppose – Tina being there, and Jonie and Mary – it was the first time I'd ever had any real friends. I didn't want to leave them."

Kate felt her eyes stinging and blinked. "So what made you go to the police when you did?"

"Jonie." Sarah cleared her throat. "Jonie arrived. She was different. She'd been abused back at home, and she knew what Peters was doing was wrong. She persuaded us to go to the police." Sarah made a small choking sound that could have been a laugh. "Chambers took my statement and I think Doherty took Tina's. We didn't know them then, but it wasn't long after that that we started getting shipped out to the hotel. I recognised him then, all right." She took a long breath in and sighed it out. "I got scared then. I knew if he was that sort of man, and he knew I'd reported Peters for abuse, then he was bound to tell him. Tina knew it too. That Doherty – he was scary. We used to see him parked outside the home sometimes, watching. Just watching."

Kate didn't think she had breathed through the whole of Sarah's speech. "What happened then?"

Sarah cleared her throat again. Her voice had grown thick, as if she had a cold. "I was all for skipping out there and then but Jonie said not to. She said she was going to the papers, she'd already contacted a journalist and she was going to meet him and give him the whole story. Then we'd be safe, because they couldn't sweep it all under the carpet anymore." She was silent for a moment and then said, with difficulty. "She said she'd spoken to him, this journo, already, and she was meeting him in two days' time. She – the next day, she'd gone. Just gone. We were told she'd run away."

"You didn't believe that?" asked Kate, who didn't believe it either.

Sarah shook her blonde head. "Of course not. Jonie wouldn't just have gone and left us all in the lurch. She had a plan, she was going to get us out of there. She said that after she'd done the interview, she was going to leave and go somewhere, somewhere where they'd never find her. And of course I said that was impossible. But she said she'd do it and fool them. She gave me a postcard to send her family, said I should post it from somewhere so they wouldn't worry."

Kate blinked, knowing that *that* was what had bothered her about Tin's conversation earlier. "Sarah, did you send that postcard that Jonie gave you when you got to Spain?"

Sarah half-smiled. "I thought that would be a good enough place." Her face clouded again. "When I got there, I don't know – I thought, how weird if Jonie actually *did* get to Spain. I was almost fantasising about it, whether I might run into her accidently or something. But I knew I wouldn't. I knew something had happened to her. She wouldn't have gone without saying goodbye, I know she wouldn't."

Kate was silent. Someone had got wind of Jonie's – Jean Tripps's - plan for exposure. Who? Godfrey Peters? Norman Chambers himself? She would put money on Kevin Doherty being the person who'd actually disposed of Jean and buried her body.

She leant forward, fixing Sarah with her eyes. "Sarah, would you be prepared to make a statement?"

Sarah looked at her with puzzlement. "What do you mean? Like Mary?"

"Yes." Kate could see that she was going to have to come clean. Bracing herself, she went on. "Sarah, I am Mary Redman's daughter, that's the absolute truth. But I will tell you something else. I'm also a police officer."

She saw the recoil, the flash of anger. Sarah was

on her feet, her posture half aggression, half fear. "A police woman? What the hell do you think you're doing? I told you everything because you said you were here from *Mary*."

"I am. I am here from Mary. I'm actually here off the record." Kate got up herself and moved backwards out of Sarah's space, holding her hands out in a reconciliatory fashion. "Sarah, listen. I'm here because the detective chief inspector of Abbeyford CID believes you. He sent me here to talk to you, to see if we could persuade you to make a statement, to see if we could help you to put these bastards behind bars. He *believes* you, and so do I. We're here to help you." Sarah was still glaring at her, one hand raised half to provoke, half to protect. "Sarah, we believe you. Help us. Help us get you the justice you deserve, that Mary – that Mum – deserves."

Kate stopped, panting.

Sarah regarded her with what looked like a slight cessation of hostility. "I want to believe you," she said, after a moment, in a low voice.

"Please, *do* believe me. I'm telling you, we're going to win this one. I give you my word. Whatever it takes, we're going to see that all those people who hurt and abused you and robbed you of your childhood, we're going to see that they pay for it. I give you my word. Whatever it takes."

Sarah stepped forward slightly. She sat down, fixing her gaze on Kate. "You'd better mean that."

"I give you my word," Kate repeated.

Chapter Twenty

THE DOOR, WITH ITS PEELING red paint, shut behind Kate and she stood for a moment in the sunshine, tipping her face up to the warmth. She felt as if she'd just emerged from underground, like some sort of tunnel-dwelling creature, as yet unused to bright light.

Shaking her head, she walked towards the car, where she could see the back of Tin's curly black head through the rear windscreen. This time, it was Kate's turn to make him jump as she opened the car door suddenly.

"Well?" asked Tin, putting his iPad away.

Kate said nothing for a moment, sliding into the driver's seat. She reached for the car keys and then stopped. She couldn't face driving just yet – her mind was fizzing with what Sarah had told her – she wouldn't have the concentration that driving a car demanded.

"Well?" prompted Tin again.

"Give me a moment," Kate said, slowly. She was

thinking furiously. There was no way that she was going to be able to tell Tin about Sarah's allegations, particularly the ones regarding Norman Chambers, not until she talked to Anderton about their next steps. She had meant every word of her impassioned speech to Sarah, but here, sitting in the car, she was coming up with a whole host of arguments as to why pursuing this was going to be a very bad idea. No. No, she was not going to let that poor woman down. If it meant that she, Kate Redman, would risk her job, then so be it. Kate heaved a big sigh and looked over at Tin. "Okay, you're not going to like this," she said.

Tin's face flickered momentarily. "Yeah?"

"Sarah made a statement, or at least she told me what had happened. But—" Kate inwardly braced herself. "I can't share that with you at the moment. I'm sorry."

"Oh, for God's sake." Tin threw his hands up in the air and flung himself out of the car in one swift movement. Shocked, Kate froze in her seat for a second before she got out herself.

Tin was standing a few feet away, his hands in his pockets, angrily rocking back and forward on the balls of his feet. Kate walked up to him warily.

"I'm sorry," she said quietly. "I wish it could be different. But I have a job to do, Tin, you know I'm constrained by that."

Tin looked at her for a long moment, his face

clearly expressing what he was thinking. Then he took his hands out of his pockets and lifted them in a gesture of resignation. "I need a bloody drink," he said and turned on his heel, making for the pub on the corner of the street.

Kate trailed after him a little uncertainly. As Tin reached the door of the pub, she became aware of her mobile ringing. She pulled it from her bag, looking at the screen. Jay's number was displayed. Kate hesitated for a moment – was it worth answering when she and Tin appeared to be in the middle of a row? – and then lifted the phone to her ear.

"Hi, Jay."

At first she thought the line was bad, the reception terrible. She could hear nothing at first but the odd muffled word. "Jay – you're breaking up—"

The line seemed to clear. Kate heard her brother's voice clearly, his tear-filled, choked, heartbroken voice. "Kate. Mum's died."

There was a second of blankness as Kate took in the words and then she was suddenly on the pavement, all the strength running out of her legs. She could hear Jay talking to her, words interspersed with sobs but she wasn't able to talk back, she couldn't say anything. Grief had lain her to waste.

Suddenly Tin was there, his arms around her, helping her up. She felt him take the phone from her hand, heard him talking to Jay, explaining who he was. She heard it all as if she were behind a sheet of thick glass, hearing it from afar. She was crying so hard she could barely see. Then Tin picked her up bodily and carried her back to the car. She felt him put her in the passenger seat and fasten the belt around her and then, though her eyes were closed, her hands hiding the world from her view, she felt the car move as Tin drove them away.

Looking back on the time between that phone call and the time where she lay on her hotel bed, crying, Kate realised that she must have moved, must have walked from the car, through the pub and up the stairs to their rooms, but she couldn't remember it. It had been erased from her memory as if a giant hand had wiped it away.

Kate lay on the bed and cried, and Tin lay beside her and held her. He didn't say anything, no platitudes or hurtful, thoughtless comments, for which she was grateful. He just lay and held her, and gradually the storm of tears stopped and she was able to lie there, her chest hitching in the aftermath of her crying fit, until the windows of the room darkened as night drew in and eventually, lulled by the warmth and nearness of Tin, worn out by emotion, Kate fell asleep.

WHEN SHE WOKE IN THE morning, Tin was still there. It seemed the most natural thing in the world to reach for him, seeking comfort. He didn't resist but whispered to her "Are you sure?" and Kate nodded, wordlessly.

Afterwards, they lay together in each other's arms. Kate could feel the sadness beginning to gather again, grief building and building in a relentless wave before she started crying again, softly this time. *Poor, poor Mum*. All the bitterness and resentment from her childhood was washed away for the moment, and Kate could only mourn for the relationship they might have had, for the few fond memories she did have of her mother. She remembered their last meeting, the final hug goodbye although she hadn't known it at the time and was glad that, at least, their final words had been those of love and tenderness.

She rang Jay, who sounded just as wrung-out and drained of tears as she herself was. She spoke to her sisters, Jade and Courtney, who were staying with Jay and Laura until the funeral. The funeral – Kate felt herself tremble at the thought of it. She supposed that she should be the one to organise it, but Jay reassured her that he and Laura would take care of the arrangements. Kate gave way, gratefully, and not for the first time thanked God that her brother had such a wonderful fiancée.

Tin had tactfully absented himself as Kate made her phone calls but he came back into the room, freshly changed and showered. Kate sat on the

ECHO

edge of the bed, slumped over, and Tin came and crouched down between her legs, putting one hand on each knee.

"Okay?" he said. There was so much concern in his voice that Kate almost started crying again but managed to control herself.

"I think so," she replied, with a watery smile. They both looked at each other. The usual slight awkwardness that might be felt after a first shared sexual experience was conspicuous in its absence. Kate felt – *safe*, that was the word. The uncertainty, the anxiety that she was used to feeling at this tentative early stage in a relationship was gone. She sighed deeply and leant forward resting her head on Tin's broad shoulder.

"Could you eat something?" he asked. "It's no problem if not..."

"No, I could," said Kate, surprised to find that she was actually hungry. She pushed herself off the bed, wobbled a little and added, "I think I really *do* need to eat something."

They made their way down to the restaurant section of the pub and found a table right at the back. Kate let Tin order for her. She was undergoing what every recently bereaved person experienced – the surprise and the anger that the world was going on much as it always had, despite the earthquake that had just taken place in her life.

She thought of what Sarah had told her yesterday and felt nothing. She knew that soon, that would change, but at that very moment, the thought of actually having to do something about it was too much. She couldn't do it. But Mary had been so brave, had been so insistent that the two of them do something about it. How could Kate let her down now? *I'm sorry, Mum*, she said to Mary in the privacy of her own head. *I won't let you down. Just let me have this one day to grieve, and then I'll carry on.*

Plates of food arrived in front of them and Kate ate what was there mechanically, tasting nothing, re-fuelling. Afterwards, the two of them went back up to Kate's room. This time there was no love-making. Kate didn't even need to say anything. Tin just laid her down on the bed, curled himself around behind her and let her drift off to sleep again, warm and comforted.

Chapter Twenty One

KATE KNOCKED AND OPENED THE door in answer to Anderton's shout.

"Kate," he said in surprise as she entered his office. "I thought you were – aren't you on compassionate leave? I was really sorry to hear about your mother."

"Thank you," murmured Kate, the usual colourless rejoinder that she'd been forced to make day in and day out for the past week. "I am but I came in because I needed to talk to you."

"Take a pew," Anderton said, indicating the chair opposite him.

"Privately," Kate said, remaining standing.

There was a moment's silence. Then Anderton said "Ah," nodded to himself and got up, reaching for his coat.

They didn't speak for the whole time they were walking to Anderton's car, or for the whole of the journey to the quiet county pub that they'd been to before, the night that Fliss had surprised them.

How long ago it seemed, Kate thought, as Anderton drew the car into a parking space at the back of the pub. How much had happened since then. She shut the car door and followed Anderton's broad back into the pub, pulling her coat more tightly around her. Despite the gradually warming spring weather, she always felt cold nowadays. Shock and emotional strain, Tin had said. Thinking of him, Kate checked her mobile almost as a reflex and looked at the last text he'd sent her, first thing that morning. No words but just a line of kisses.

Comforted slightly, she made her way to the snug at the back of the pub whilst Anderton got their drinks. A small part of her was dreading the upcoming conversation, but most of her just felt empty. Empty, sad and lost. Magda had told her that was normal, that there were distinct stages of grief to be worked through, but at the moment, Kate felt like she didn't have the energy for working through anything. The one thing that was keeping her going was the promise she'd made to Sarah Smith and to the ghosts of her mother, Jean Tripp, Tina Fetterden and Jane Moor.

"So," Anderton said. "How are you? The funeral's on Friday, isn't it?"

Kate nodded. "Would you mind very much if we didn't talk about that, sir?"

Anderton looked slightly uncomfortable. "Of course, of course." There was a short moment of silence whilst he sipped his pint and Kate tried to gather the energy to speak. "So...?"

Kate drew a deep breath. "I managed to make contact with one of the girls who made an accusation of sexual abuse against the manager of Marhaven, Godfrey Peters. Her name is – well, was, she's changed it several times since then – was Sarah Smith."

Anderton nodded. "Yes, I remember."

Kate continued. "She opened up to me because I'm - I *am* Mary's daughter." She managed to hide the jab of pain that speaking her mother's name brought her. "She trusted me enough to tell me all about what used to go on at Marhaven." She explained to Anderton some of the accusations that Sarah had made, the sex parties with underage girls, the sexual abuse at the home itself. At that point, she didn't mention any names.

Anderton listened to it all. "Is she credible?" was his first question, when Kate paused for breath.

Kate nodded. "Yes. Yes, I believe so. She's very suspicious, very hostile to the police because of what happened—" She stopped herself for a moment. "I'll get onto that in a minute," she said, a trifle awkwardly. "But despite all that, I think she'd be prepared to make a statement, to testify in court if there's a chance of a conviction."

Anderton raised his eyebrows. "So she's named a suspect, or several suspects, who are still living?"

Kate nodded, swallowed to try and get some moisture into her dry mouth. "Yes. Yes, she has." She paused, gathered her courage together with both hands. "One of the suspects she's named as complicit and involved in a paedophile ring operating at the time, in the seventies, is – is known to you already." She heard the dread in her tone, saw it mirrored in Anderton's apprehensive face. "It's Norman Chambers."

In the echoing silence that followed, Kate kept her eyes fixed on Anderton's face. She saw something there, just a flash of an emotion that, when the full impact struck her, she gasped in horror. Anderton – some small part of Anderton— was not surprised. Kate raised a shaking hand to her mouth. "You knew," she said, through paper-dry lips.

Anderton leant forward and grabbed her arm, shaking his head. "No. No! I did not *know*." She could see him trying to recover his poise and winced beneath the tightening hand on her arm. "You just gave me a hell of a shock, that's all." He caught sight of Kate's increasingly pained expression and snatched his hand back from her arm with an exclamation. "Sorry. It's just – my God, Kate. Norman Chambers." His voice dropped almost down to a whisper.

Kate sat back, keeping her eyes fixed on his face. She knew she hadn't misread that first flash of emotion. "You weren't surprised. Not really surprised. Are you really, honestly telling me that you didn't know what he was like?"

Anderton eyed her. "I'd be bloody careful about what you're implying, DS Redman," he said, in a not very friendly voice. "Yes, I'd just tread a wee bit carefully with what you're implying."

If he was trying to frighten her, it wasn't working. Dimly, Kate thought that she was too wrung-out emotionally to be bothered about being frightened. "I'm not implying anything. All I'm saying is that when I mentioned his name, in connection with a *paedophile ring*, for a second, you looked as though it wasn't news to you. Are you telling me I'm wrong?"

Anderton sat back too, mirroring her posture. His eyes never left her face. "You don't just go and accuse the former chief superintendent of this county of paedophilia, Kate."

"Oh, don't I?" said Kate, sarcasm dripping from every word. "Why not, if that's what he is?"

They eyed one another for a long moment. Then Anderton sighed and broke the eye contact. He seemed to sag a little in his seat. "There was nothing concrete," he said, quietly. "Nothing but rumours. And not many of those. Just a few jokes flying around, you know, when I first joined, that he liked them young. It was the eighties, Kate, people made jokes about sexy schoolgirls and things like that." Kate rolled her eyes in disgust and Anderton held up a hand. "All right, it was wrong. I get that, I'm not denying that. But when you asked me if I knew, then if what is being alleged is true, then of course I bloody didn't. What do you take me for? I've got three daughters of my own, you know. Do you think I relish the fact that, if this *is* true, one of my long-term colleagues, former boss and family friend is that sort of man? Do you?"

"No," Kate said. "Of course not. I'm not stupid. But given what we know, what else can we do?" Anderton looked away, into the depths of his pint. Kate repeated "What else can we do?"

There was another long moment of silence. Then Anderton cleared his throat and spoke. "We could – we could do nothing."

Kate felt the bottom of her stomach drop, as if she were standing in a plummeting lift. "What?"

Anderton didn't answer for a moment. "If we go ahead, this is going to bring up one hell of a shitstorm, Kate. Do you know how many cases we'll have to re-examine if it turns out that Norman is – is guilty?"

"*If?*" said Kate, trying to moisten her dry mouth.

Anderton took no notice. "All these things have been buried for so long. Do we – do you want the responsibility of raking it all up again?"

Kate clasped her shaking hands together in her lap. "I can't believe I'm hearing this. Are you seriously saying we should just forget it? Just let it all – just rake it under the carpet again?"

Anderton was still refusing to meet her eye. "All I'm saying is that perhaps we should think about what we'd be doing. Whether it would actually be for the best."

Kate sat still, clasping her hands and staring at nothing over the table. Her heart thumped. She thought of her mother, looking at her over the rim of the oxygen mask, the frantic appeal in her eyes. She thought of her mother's bravery; in choking out her statement, struggling against her failing lungs because she knew that she had to do it. Giving that statement had probably hastened her death, Kate realised. She sat up a little straighter and drew back her shoulders.

"Sir," she said. "I gave my word to the victims of the Marhaven home that I would see this case through until justice was done. Now, I want that justice to be achieved through our investigation."

"Right," said Anderton. "But—"

Kate went on, talking over him. "If you won't help me on this, if you refuse to see it through, then I'm afraid you leave me no choice."

Anderton's eyes narrowed. "*Meaning?*"

Kate swallowed. "I will take all the evidence I've gathered so far and I will take it to the press."

There was a moment of silence. The hubbub from the public bar out in the corridor seemed to fade away for a moment. Kate could feel the small hard semi-circles of her fingernails digging into the palms of her hands.

Anderton spoke then, quite softly. "You realise

that if you did that, it would be the end of your career in the police force?"

"I'm aware of that fact," said Kate, trying not to let her voice tremble.

"You'd risk that?" Anderton's eyes searched her face. "You'd throw away all those years of sacrifice and hard work, for crimes that were committed forty years ago?"

Kate squared her shoulders. "Yes. I would. Because it's the right thing to do." She looked him in the eye and although she spoke softly, the passion in her voice made it vibrate. "Because if we turn a blind eye now, what happens forty years into the future? How many children are out there *now*, being abused and not being believed? Throw the historic cases open, make it known, and perhaps we can stop it from happening again. Can't you see that?"

They both regarded each other in silence. Kate held her breath. Then Anderton shook his head slowly, with sadness. "I can't, Kate. We don't have the evidence."

"Oh, *bollocks*." Anger finally made itself felt. Kate leant forward and smacked one fist against the table top. "We've got credible victim statements, we've got the journalist who was contacted by the murder victim, we've got *plenty* of evidence. Put an appeal out for other victims and people will come forward. Set up a report line for victims to contact us. You *know* there's more out there, you *know* as soon as one person comes forward and breaks the silence, others will follow. There'll be plenty of people out there who knew what went on at Marhaven, so don't tell me that we don't – or we won't – have the evidence." She breathed in sharply and sat back, flexing the hand that she'd banged on the table. She looked Anderton straight in the eye. "You're just too much of a bloody coward to see it through."

She pushed her chair back from the table, snatched up her bag and turned to go, sick at heart. What the hell – she was fired anyway. She was at the doorway when Anderton spoke.

"Kate. Kate."

She stopped but didn't turn around. She heard Anderton get up and walk towards her but kept her face turned away until he appeared around the corner of her vision, moving around until he was facing her and blocking the doorway.

"Was your mother proud of you?" he asked.

"I don't know," said Kate, tightly. "Probably not."

"Well," Anderton said. "She should have been."

Kate blinked away the tears that rushed to her eyes. She stood, clutching her arms across her body, knowing that she should say something, but for that moment, she was just clean out of words. They were all gone, swept away by the rush of emotion.

"Come on," Anderton said. "Sit back down. Let's discuss what we're going to do first."

"First?" asked Kate, finally daring to look at him. She thought of industrial tribunals, getting a lawyer, finding out who her union representative should be.

"Yes," Anderton said. "We should probably start with setting up the help line, like you said. And after that, proceeding with the interview, under caution, of Norman Chambers. Don't you think?"

Chapter Twenty Two

ON FRIDAY MORNING, KATE REGARDED herself in the mirror of the women's toilets at Abbeyford Station. She looked horribly pale, she thought, but then top-to-toe black never had suited her. She pinched her cheeks, trying to get some colour back into them, and smoothed her hair back for the fifteenth time that day. Displacement activity, she knew that. She straightened the lapels of her jacket, took a deep breath and turned away from the mirror.

"Why are you going into work *today*, of all days?" Jay had asked her that very morning. Kate had muttered something about needing to check on the investigation but she didn't really know the answer herself. There was some comfort in being back here, that was the sad thing. She'd seen the new bank of telephones and the specially trained staff who were seated by them, ready for the calls. Kate looked in again as she passed the room where they were situated. One of the women was already talking to someone on the phone. Kate nodded in quiet satisfaction and made her way to the station exit.

She had to pass through the canteen on the way and found her gaze drawn to the television that hung on one wall. It was always tuned to one of the twenty-four hour news stations. Kate passed it and stopped suddenly, hearing what they were currently reporting on. She stood watching the screen, clutching her elbows across her body.

The reporter was a young woman, barely mid-twenties, with a fall of long, glossy chestnut hair. She was standing outside of the Abbeyford County Court building – Kate recognised the entrance. She concentrated on what the young woman was saying – it wasn't news to her, but it was the first time she'd seen it reported in the press.

"Former chief superintendent of the North West Somerset Police Force, Norman Chambers, today appeared in court charged with the possession of over a thousand images of child sexual abuse. The pictures were found on his home computer after police raided his house in connection with Operation Echo, the ongoing investigation into the historic abuse cases, centred around the Marhaven care home in the nineteen seventies and eighties..."

Kate blew out her cheeks. She watched Norman Chambers being handed into the back of a police car, on his way to – where? Home? Prison? The latter, probably. Kate hoped so.

"North West Somerset Police have confirmed that several historic cases will be re-opened, given the involvement of Chambers and his deputy, disgraced ex-officer, Kevin Doherty. Doherty, who died in nineteen eighty, is implicated in the murder of teenager Jean Tripp, who was also a ward of the Marhaven care home—"

Kate shifted from one foot to the other. She knew she should be going but there was something grimly fascinating about seeing everything play out on the small screen in front of her. She glanced at her watch, caught her breath at the time.

The young reporter was still speaking. "Police have set up a victim support help line in connection with Operation Echo, for anyone who might have something to report in connection with the cases under investigation. The number is—"

Kate finally turned away. Holding her bouncing handbag against her, she ran through the station and out the front door, emerging into sunlight so brilliant that for a moment she stopped, dazzled. Once she'd blinked her way back to clarity, she saw Tin behind the wheel of his car, waiting for her at the foot of the steps, the engine idling. She raised a hand and saw him smile in return, a more subdued smile than his normal wide grin, fitting with the solemnity of the day.

There were a lot of people standing about on the pavement. As Kate made her way down the steps, she recognised them, all of a sudden, stopping dead and blinking. There was Anderton, in black, and Olbeck next to him, and Rav and Theo and Jane and Fliss...

"What's going on?" asked Kate, staring at her colleagues.

"Well, you didn't think we'd let you go to the funeral on your own, did you?" replied Anderton. He tugged at the lapels of his black jacket, straightening it.

"Don't be silly," added Olbeck. He reached Kate's side and pulled her into a hug, kissing the top of her head.

Kate swallowed past the huge blockage in her throat. "Thank you," she said, in a watery voice, once she was able to speak.

"So, we're following you, yeah?" asked Theo, twirling his car keys around one long forefinger. Jane and Fliss were obviously travelling with him. Rav and Olbeck arranged themselves behind Anderton.

There was a subdued shout from Tin, who had got out of the driver's seat. "What's the hold up? Oh—" he said, once he'd realised what was going on.

Kate gave Olbeck's arm a squeeze as she walked past him on her way to the car. "I've finally finished the speech. I hope it's okay."

Olbeck gave a short laugh. "My God, Kate, you don't think Jeff and I are worried about that now, do you?" He moved aside to let her past him. "But, thank you," he added. "I'm sure it'll be great."

Kate gave him a relieved smile. She slid into the

passenger seat beside Tin, and he leant over and kissed her. "All right?" he asked, with obvious concern.

"I'll be fine," said Kate. She glanced in the rear view mirror and saw her colleagues getting into their own vehicles, ready to follow her. "I'm sure I'll be fine."

Tin said nothing but he gave her leg a squeeze before putting the car in gear. The vehicle moved off from the kerb, followed by the two others behind it; driving off towards the funeral, through the golden morning sunshine.

BACK AT THE STATION, IN the room where the telephone bank stood, the phones continued to ring. One of the operators picked up the receiver and spoke in her calmest and most professional tone.

"Operation Echo Reporting Line. How may I help you?"

A woman's voice on the other end of the line, hesitant. The operator listened, spoke gently in reply, made notes on her writing pad. Around her, the lines trilled and voices rose into the air like smoke.

"Operation Echo—"

"Operation Echo Reporting Line—"

"Hello, you've reached the Operation Echo Reporting Line. How can I help you?"

THE END

Enjoyed this book? An honest review left at Amazon, Goodreads, Shelfari and LibraryThing is always welcome and really important for indie authors. The more reviews an independently published book has, the easier it is to market it and find new readers.

Want some more of Celina Grace's work for free? Subscribers to her mailing list get a free digital copy of Requiem (A Kate Redman Mystery: Book 2), a free digital copy of A Prescription for Death (The Asharton Manor Mysteries Book 2) and a free PDF copy of her short story collection A Blessing From The Obeah Man.

Requiem
(A Kate Redman Mystery: Book 2)

WHEN THE BODY OF TROUBLED teenager Elodie Duncan is pulled from the river in Abbeyford, the case is at first assumed to be a straightforward suicide. Detective Sergeant Kate Redman is shocked to discover that she'd met the victim the night before her death, introduced by Kate's younger brother Jay. As the case develops, it becomes clear that Elodie was murdered. A talented young musician, Elodie had been keeping some strange company and was hiding her own dark secrets.

As the list of suspects begin to grow, so do the questions. What is the significance of the painting Elodie modelled for? Who is the man who was seen with her on the night of her death? Is there any connection with another student's death at the exclusive musical college that Elodie attended?

As Kate and her partner Detective Sergeant Mark Olbeck attempt to unravel the mystery, the dark undercurrents of the case threaten those whom Kate holds most dear...

A Prescription for Death
(The Asharton Manor Mysteries: Book 2) – a novella

"I had a surge of kinship the first time
I saw the manor, perhaps because
we'd both seen better days."

IT IS 1947. ASHARTON MANOR, once one of the most beautiful stately homes in the West Country, is now a convalescent home for former soldiers. Escaping the devastation of post-war London is Vivian Holt, who moves to the nearby village and begins to volunteer as a nurse's aide at the manor. Mourning the death of her soldier husband, Vivian finds solace in her new friendship with one of the older patients, Norman Winter, someone who has served his country in both world wars. Slowly, Vivian's heart begins to heal, only to be torn apart when she arrives for work one day to be told that Norman is dead.

It seems a straightforward death, but is it? Why did a particular photograph disappear from Norman's possessions after his death? Who is the sinister figure who keeps following Vivian? Suspicion and doubts begin to grow and when another death occurs, Vivian begins to realise that the war may be over but the real battle is just beginning...

A Blessing From The Obeah Man

Dare you read on? Horrifying, scary, sad and thought-provoking, this short story collection will take you on a macabre journey. In the titular story, a honeymooning couple take a wrong turn on their trip around Barbados. The Mourning After brings you a shiversome story from a suicidal teenager. In Freedom Fighter, an unhappy middle-aged man chooses the wrong day to make a bid for freedom, whereas Little Drops of Happiness and Wave Goodbye are tales of darkness from sunny Down Under. Strapping Lass and The Club are for those who prefer, shall we say, a little meat to the story...

JUST GO TO CELINA'S BLOG on writing and self-publishing to sign up. It's quick, easy and free. Be the first to be informed of promotions, giveaways, new releases and subscriber-only benefits by subscribing to her (occasional) newsletter.

http://www.celinagrace.com

Twitter:
@celina__grace

Facebook:
http://www.facebook.com/authorcelinagrace

More books by Celina Grace...

Hushabye
(A Kate Redman Mystery: Book 1)

ON THE FIRST DAY OF her new job in the West Country, Detective Sergeant Kate Redman finds herself investigating the kidnapping of Charlie Fullman, the newborn son of a wealthy entrepreneur and his trophy wife. It seems a straightforward case... but as Kate and her fellow officer Mark Olbeck delve deeper, they uncover murky secrets and multiple motives for the crime.

Kate finds the case bringing up painful memories of her own past secrets. As she confronts the truth about herself, her increasing emotional instability threatens both her hard-won career success and the possibility that they will ever find Charlie Fullman alive...

Hushabye is the book that introduces Detective Sergeant Kate Redman. Available as a FREE download from Amazon Kindle.

Imago
(A Kate Redman Mystery: Book 3)

"THEY DON'T FEAR ME, QUITE the opposite. It makes it twice as fun... I know the next time will be soon, I've learnt to recognise the signs. I think I even know who it will be. She's oblivious of course, just as she should be. All the time, I watch and wait and she has no idea, none at all. And why would she? I'm disguised as myself, the very best disguise there is."

A known prostitute is found stabbed to death in a shabby corner of Abbeyford. Detective Sergeant Kate Redman and her partner Detective Sergeant Olbeck take on the case, expecting to have it wrapped up in a matter of days. Kate finds herself distracted by her growing attraction to her boss, Detective Chief Inspector Anderton – until another woman's body is found, with the same knife wounds. And then another one after that, in a matter of days.

Forced to confront the horrifying realisation that a serial killer may be preying on the vulnerable women of Abbeyford, Kate, Olbeck and the team find themselves in a race against time to unmask a terrifying murderer, who just might be hiding in plain sight...

Buy Imago on Amazon, available now.

Snarl
(A Kate Redman Mystery: Book 4)

A RESEARCH LABORATORY OPENS ON THE outskirts of Abbeyford, bringing with it new people, jobs, prosperity and publicity to the area – as well as a mob of protesters and animal rights activists. The team at Abbeyford police station take this new level of civil disorder in their stride – until a fatal car bombing of one of the laboratory's head scientists means more drastic measures must be taken...

Detective Sergeant Kate Redman is struggling to come to terms with being back at work after long period of absence on sick leave; not to mention the fact that her erstwhile partner Olbeck has now been promoted above her. The stakes get even higher as a multiple murder scene is uncovered and a violent activist is implicated in the crime. Kate and the team must put their lives on the line to expose the murderer and untangle the snarl of accusations, suspicions and motives.

Snarl is the fourth Kate Redman Mystery from crime writer Celina Grace, author of Hushabye, Requiem and Imago. Available now from Amazon.

Chimera
(A Kate Redman Mystery: Book 5)

THE WEST COUNTRY TOWN OF Abbeyford is celebrating its annual pagan festival, when the festivities are interrupted by the discovery of a very decomposed body. Soon, several other bodies are discovered but is it a question of foul play or are these deaths from natural causes?

It's a puzzle that Detective Sergeant Kate Redman and the team could do without, caught up as they are in investigating an unusual series of robberies. Newly single again, Kate also has to cope with her upcoming Inspector exams and a startling announcement from her friend and colleague DI Mark Olbeck...

When a robbery goes horribly wrong, Kate begins to realise that the two cases might be linked. She must use all her experience and intelligence to solve a serious of truly baffling crimes which bring her up against an old adversary from her past...

Available from Amazon now.

CELINA GRACE'S PSYCHOLOGICAL THRILLER, **LOST Girls** is also available from Amazon:

Twenty-three years ago, Maudie Sampson's childhood friend Jessica disappeared on a family holiday in Cornwall. She was never seen again.

In the present day, Maudie is struggling to come to terms with the death of her wealthy father, her increasingly fragile mental health and a marriage that's under strain. Slowly, she becomes aware that there is someone following her: a blonde woman in a long black coat with an intense gaze. As the woman begins to infiltrate her life, Maudie realises no one else appears to be able to see her.

Is Maudie losing her mind? Is the woman a figment of her imagination or does she actually exist? Have the sins of the past caught up with Maudie's present...or is there something even more sinister going on?

Lost Girls is a novel from the author of The House on Fever Street: a dark and convoluted tale which proves that nothing can be taken for granted and no-one is as they seem.

Currently available exclusively from Amazon.

THE HOUSE ON FEVER STREET is the first psychological thriller from Celina Grace.

Thrown together in the aftermath of the London bombings of 2005, Jake and Bella embark on a passionate and intense romance. Soon Bella is living with Jake in his house on Fever Street, along with his sardonic brother Carl and Carl's girlfriend, the beautiful but chilly Veronica.

As Bella tries to come to terms with her traumatic experience, her relationship with Jake also becomes a source of unease. Why do the housemates never go into the garden? Why does Jake have such bad dreams and such explosive outbursts of temper?

Bella is determined to understand the man she loves but as she uncovers long-buried secrets, is she putting herself back into mortal danger?

The House on Fever Street is the first psychological thriller from writer Celina Grace - a chilling study of the violent impulses that lurk beneath the surfaces of everyday life.

Shortlisted for the 2006 Crime Writers' Association Debut Dagger Award.

Currently available exclusively from Amazon.

Extra Special Thanks Are Due To My Wonderful Advance Readers Team...

THESE ARE MY 'SUPER READERS' who are kind enough to beta read my books, point out my more ridiculous mistakes, spot any typos that have slipped past my editor and best of all, write honest reviews in exchange for advance copies of my work. Many, many thanks to you all. Special mention goes to Margaret Gardiner, June Donnelly, Gina, Bonnie Bunge, Helen Drye, Deanne Wimberley, Marian Grandy, Beth Bruik, Alan Pease, Kathleen Charon, Valerie Cobbs, Shannon Watz, Rick Felix, Alexandra Ragle, Fleur Wilkinson, Verlie Williams, Roxanne Loveday, Janet C Clarke, Anne Dannerolle, Denise Grzesiak, Alan Pease, Rosemary Earl, Maureen Vincent-Northam, Karen Ford, Teresa Jones, Cathy Rock, Marianna Roberg, Margie Nelson, Sue Reid, Dave Floyd, Shauna Taylor, Myra Duffy, Andrea T, Caithlin Barry, Patricia George-Lezama, Michelle Judge, Denise Zendel, Jackie Montgomery, Donna Wolz, Kim Davy.

If you fancy being an Advance Reader, just drop me a line at celina@celinagrace.com and I'll add you to the list. It's completely free, and you can unsubscribe at any time.

ACKNOWLEDGEMENTS

Many thanks to all the following splendid souls:

Chris Howard for the brilliant cover designs; Andrea Harding for editing and proofreading; Kathy McConnell for extra proofreading and beta reading; lifelong Schlockers and friends David Hall, Ben Robinson and Alberto Lopez; Ross McConnell for advice on police procedure and for also being a great brother; Kathleen and Pat McConnell, Anthony Alcock, Naomi White, Mo Argyle, Lee Benjamin, Bonnie Wede, Sherry and Amali Stoute, Cheryl Lucas, Georgia Lucas-Going, Steven Lucas, Loletha Stoute and Harry Lucas, Helen Parfect, Helen Watson, Emily Way, Sandy Hall, Kristýna Vosecká, Katie D'Arcy and of course my wonderful and ever-loving Chris, Mabel, Jethro and Isaiah.

Printed in Great Britain
by Amazon

58076197R00148